I Wanna Hear It Again

Tales of Home and the World

W. E. Smith

The following is a work of fiction. Names, characters, places, and incidents are either products of the author's imagination or used fictiously. Any resemblance to actual events, locales, or persons living or dead is entirely coincidental.

Also by W. E. Smith

Novels

Be True to Your Tribe

Tanaki on the Shore

Ver Sacrum, or Heaven Help Us All

Bal Harbour

I've Got a Right to Sing the Blues

Short Stories

He on Honeydew Hath Fed

I Wanna Hear It Again

Tales of Home and the World

Table of Contents

Sea Oats: A Photograph

I was cruising along A1A with the beach to my left: slowly, because it was a fine scene, and I wanted to take it all in. It was my last day in Florida. The sun, still not far off the horizon, spread a golden sheen across the surface of the ocean. Waves lapped against the shoreline, and a couple of freighters sat serenely in the offing. A low wall separated the beach from the road. Over its top I saw the tasseled sea oats waving in the breeze.

I pulled over to take this photograph—the one sitting here on my desk—although Rick was waiting for me to return with the Cherokee and drop little Kim at school. I was on my annual visit from up north, and Rick had put the Jeep at my disposal. He and Sharon were using the old pickup to get around.

Rick had been elected to the city commission a couple of years earlier, in an upset victory over a former state senator with a raft of connections and a sizable war chest. He was new to politics. He'd gotten involved in the civic association over pollutants which fouled the waters of the canal bordering his quiet, working-class community, leading his neighbors in chanting delegations to hearings at the municipal building.

The sea oats were one of the controversies Rick had gotten involved in since the election. This guy Joe Chambers said that he was ruining the beach. The local papers even quoted Chambers:

"Rick Baxter is ruining the Henderson beachfront,"

Chambers said. "I've been here thirty years, and I've never seen anything like it."

The papers love a controversy.

Ecology experts consulted by the commission had recommended the sea oats to prevent erosion of the shoreline. Like all barrier islands, the one on which Fort Henderson was built is a structure not designed by nature for longevity; which may be fine for nature, but not for the owners of the upscale hotels and condos that stud the city's glamorous beachfront. By some quirk of electoral fate, Rick represented that part of the city— its wealthiest—along with his own more modest neighborhood.

Joe Chambers stood up at a commission meeting. He said that if the ecologists' plans were put into effect, the view of the ocean from A1A, the same view I had stopped to photograph, would be obliterated. Chambers' remarks were not without foundation. The purpose of the sea oats was to create dunes. With the stabilizing effects of the vegetation, the dunes would grow in size, like life forms themselves, into large mounds all along that strip of beach. When this came to pass, the dunes would indeed, as Joe Chambers averred, block the view of the ocean from the road.

"Let him get out of his damn car and walk to the beach if he wants to see the ocean," Rick said.

It didn't help that Chambers was already upset over some new construction projects along the shore. Rick had supported height exceptions for a couple of developments, because he believed that the city's economy depended on the beachfront's vitality.

"Rick Baxter is ruining the Henderson beachfront," Chambers stood up and said, right there at a commission meeting in front of everyone.

"Of course the bozo's own condo got an exception," Rick

told me, pointing out the looming high-rise as we drove along the shore one day. "It's always NIMBY."

It was hard to conceive, whatever the merits of the issue, that my younger brother, Ricky Baxter, could be capable of doing anything so consequential as ruining an entire beach resort. If it were true, I would have been considerably impressed.

****

Since we are only eleven months apart, we were closer than other brothers might be. We shared a bedroom until my sixteenth year, when Doug went off to college and vacated his room in the basement. Our twin beds stood parallel, a couple of feet apart, and as boys we lay awake nights, obliging one another to give a full accounting of the day at school.

"Then what happened?" we'd say.

"And then what happened?"

As we entered adolescence, however, the sibling rivalry that had always subordinated itself to our sense of camaraderie came to the fore. Rick developed more quickly than I, and before I had my first wet dream he was using a razor. He was the youngest of us three boys, and had gotten used to his position at the bottom of the pecking order—or perhaps it was only Doug and I who had gotten used to his position at the bottom of the pecking order. In any case, nature worked an odd trick, investing him with the musculature of a grown man by the time he was thirteen. Doug, always sagacious, realized that the jig was up and quit picking on him. As the oldest brother, he could afford to take an Olympian stance. He had other things to attend to, motorcycles, girlfriends, college plans.

I had to learn the hard way.

Rick must have been aware of his new assets, because as

his upper body followed its astounding course of development, stimulated by daily bouts of weightlifting after school, he began—subtly at first, and then always more blatantly—to challenge the nature of our relationship. It began with elder rights, things like riding shotgun in the car, or choosing the channel on the TV set. Doug's absorption in more mature interests had left a power vacuum as regards these sorts of boyhood squabbles.

As he gained confidence, and compared his budding torso to my skinny, boyish body, he ratcheted up his assault on my precarious dominance. He progressed from challenges over concrete issues to a more general taunting, a constant effort to prick the bubble of my self-designated superiority. He stood between our beds, in the space that had conveyed so many boyhood confidences, and challenged my masculinity with lewd remarks.

'There it is, Wuss,' he'd say, holding his stumpy wiener in his hand. "Go ahead and suck it.'

Of course he was fed up with the ribbing I gave him over the acne cream he caked onto his face each night like a tragic mask.

We had both taken up wrestling in school, following Doug's footsteps, and the sport provided an arena for working out our evolving relationship. Rick outweighed me, and now possessed, as I've said, a marked advantage in strength. Yet when we practiced our moves at home, I was still able to contain his compact form with my gangly, flexible limbs. I now realize that Rick allowed this state of affairs to continue longer than was necessary. I couldn't admit it to myself, but he refused to bring all of his strength to bear when we wrestled.

Never since has anyone been so solicitous of my *amour propre*.

But every lie eventually falls of its own weight, as they say, and the disconnect between my conception of our relationship and reality could not continue indefinitely. As it happened, one bright summer afternoon we got into some ridiculous argument in the yard. No one was around but the two of us. The sun beat down relentlessly on the wide lawn where we had played countless ball games, in season and out. I don't remember who made the first move, but we were soon on the earth, tugging at taut limbs, arching necks and backs, grinding toes into the fresh grass. This went on for some time, but the long and short of it is he wound up on top. I was on all fours, in the classic "down" position of scholastic wrestling. He grasped my elbow firmly with one hand, and his other arm was wrapped around my waist like a steel clamp.

"Watcha gonna do now, Wuss?" he said, only slightly winded.

"I'm gonna kill you," I said, wriggling within the minimal leeway his death grip allowed.

"How're you gonna do that?" He was enjoying himself immensely.

I tried to throw my head back, hoping to strike him in the face, but it was no good. He was able to hold his face well away from my body and still exert enough force to keep me immobilized. Sweat dripped from my forehead onto the lawn.

"I'll let you up if you promise not to hit me," he said.

I told him to go to hell, but he let me up anyway. We strutted around the yard, circling warily and exchanging insults. Neither of us was ready to put the issue to the test again: I, because I could conceive of nothing to achieve a better result, and Rick (I can only speculate here) because he was giddy about the psychological barrier he had crossed, maybe even uncertain about whether he liked having crossed it.

We let the issue rest for some time, as we both had other things to occupy ourselves with. Of course I kept razzing him about the acne cream that, besides looking bizarre, put off a rotten odor of sulfur. Meanwhile he honed his verbal challenges to my yet-to-be-acquired manhood.

****

Did any of this come to mind as I drove along the Henderson beachfront last winter and stopped to take this photograph, the one propped here on my desk? Not really. Many years have passed, and my relationship with Rick has long since recovered the easy feel of our earliest years. But as I contemplate these young sea oats struggling to find their places in the sun, I find myself engulfed by long-buried memories of my brother, and puzzling over the distances that still separate us.

At the end of his senior college year Rick was struck by a life-threatening illness and spent months convalescing at our father's Baltimore townhouse. When he was finally up and about it was the dead of winter, so he decided on a trip to Florida to find the sun and warmth he intuitively knew would complete his healing. He was offered a job managing the cheap motel where he put up (a dive for hookers and junkies, really) and decided to stay. In the years that followed he worked his way through Henderson's tourist economy, marrying his Sharon and building a thriving landscaping business along the way.

The day before I ended last winter's visit I helped him and Sharon with one of their landscaping jobs. They had been contracted to plant several coconut palms, along with myriad smaller plants, in front of an old beachfront hotel. Rick was oblivious to the raw wind that drove rain into our faces as we—Rick and I along with a few hired hands—muscled the palm trees, with their massive root balls, off a flatbed truck and through a muddy garden to the holes we had dug to accommodate them.

"Man, you're a real monster, Bro," Rick said after we slid

the last of the trees into its hole and back-filled it with wet, dark earth. "Did you see the way he maneuvered that mother?" he said to Sharon. She was tamping down soil with a shovel.

He is still vastly stronger than me.

The finishing touch of the installation was a flattened boulder, dusky tan, that was to be placed in the middle of the triangular planting bed. Though the palms were lovely, their delicate fronds waving over the host of smaller plants Sharon had positioned with care, it was the boulder that would anchor all of that ethereal loveliness, keep it from floating away . . .

When the boulder arrived, Rick marched over to the flatbed truck, with a rickety-looking crane and winch attached, that was idling in front of the hotel. His head was bent against the pelting rain that a rising wind was driving across the street in broad sheets. Though it was cold for Florida, he wore only a pair of shorts and a plastic windbreaker. The driver came out of the cab and hopped onto the bed of the truck. He encircled the large boulder with a heavy chain, hooked the chain to the winch, and returned to the cab. After a moment, with a low grinding noise, the boulder began to rise unsteadily. It swayed at the end of its chain as the driver attempted to maneuver it to where it could be lowered onto a waiting dolly. Rick rushed in to stabilize the massive stone, but the rest of us hung back. We were not merely leery of getting close to the boulder's crushing weight, but uncertain of the entire crane and winch arrangement.

"Be careful, Bro," I called through the rain, knowing that he would pay me no mind. Like the crane, many of Rick's arrangements in Florida possessed a jury-rigged appearance to us up north, but he always seemed to work things out.

Deftly shuffling back and forth on the pavement, he grappled the boulder with his powerful arms, guiding it towards the dolly with brute will. He maneuvered it onto the conveyance, and then I and the other men helped him wheel it into position at the center of the bed. When everything was finished, I took a photograph of him and little Kim in front of the artificial Eden we had created, an image I took to be emblematic of the life my brother had built for himself in the Sunshine State.

****

I can't leave off from this portrait of Rick—this family snapshot, if you will—without describing our last, and decisive, physical struggle. After our stalemate in the yard, the issue of bragging rights lay dormant for several months. We each had our friends and interests. We were trying to grow up.

But Vietnam was reaching its peak. Race riots flared across the country. Violence was in the very air we breathed.

We were in the basement, that chthonic lair where we gathered evenings to watch the glowing tube, played cards or board games, or hung during summer vacation to escape the outdoors heat. Had we come in from the yard, where we were fighting over a ball game? Were we arguing over the television? Or had I cheated him in poker or Monopoly? It doesn't really matter. What was needed was a pretext, a casus belli. With our standoff in the yard a line had been crossed, but not far enough to be definitive. We had grown up accustomed to a pecking order, a system of dominance and submission that began with our father, ran through Doug and then on to the two of us.

Who would be next in line?

By the time we got to the bathroom it was a knock-down, drag-out affair. I don't know how we ended up in the shower stall. We were grappling one another, trying to get our punches in. There was hardly room to stand up.

Sea Oats: A Photograph

There was no backing away.

We grappled and slugged, with little quarter given on either side, until I thrust my right thumb into a pressure point in his left armpit and pressed with all my strength. This dirty trick, which I had learned from a neighborhood kid—a karate move used by special forces in 'Nam, he told me—gave me the upper hand, and using the leverage it afforded, I drove Rick vengefully against the wall. The chrome handles for adjusting the water were on that side of the shower stall, each with three pointed fins like the ones on the back of a '57 Chevy. Rick began to yelp when his back pushed into the sharp fixtures, and he stopped struggling.

"Dammit," he screamed, "you're hurting me!"

When I saw the tears welling in his eyes I let him go. He slipped out of the shower stall and strutted through the laundry room and into the back yard, arching his back with the painful wounds that appeared like crimson hieroglyphics between his shoulder blades.

I followed behind.

"You're a bastard," he said through stifled tears.

"I didn't mean to . . ."

It's true, I hadn't meant to actually injure him, but I was determined to protect my pride from the blow of being displaced in the family pecking order by a younger brother. If anything was proven, it was that I was willing to go to greater lengths (or sink to deeper depths) to preserve my position, than he was to occupy it. Of course it was absurd, which I realized as I followed him around the yard, groping for something to say to make it better. In fact, moving through the blinding glare of that summer afternoon, a resolution formed in my mind that shortly grew into a fixed principle: I would never fight with him again. It bothered me too much to see him, hurt and bleeding, hobbling around the yard.

"You're a bastard."

The worst of it is, he probably could have kicked my butt if he really wanted to. I guess he realized there was more at stake for me, and was willing to let it go at that.

We never fought again, which was a good thing, as we needed each other's friendship more than ever over the coming years, when we faced our parents' divorce and its manifold dislocations. Of course we had our squabbles, but somehow a corner was turned in that cramped shower stall, a turning that allowed us to retrieve the natural camaraderie we had enjoyed as boys.

****

I sit here looking at this photograph, the one with the sea oats. I think about Rick, the years that have gone by, and the life he's built for himself in Florida. I suppose he had to move away. How could he have thrived, always solicitous of the fragile prides of three older males? He's not the kind to bear a grudge, at least, and always seems happiest on those too rare occasions when we all find ourselves together again.

I also think of that guy Joe Chambers, and his complaints against Rick. I figure he would appreciate this photograph: the wide Atlantic and a clear blue sky; the early sun laying a golden sheen across the water; and in the foreground, a couple of palm trees, their fronds shuffling in the breeze. He might feel a certain irritation on perceiving, just creeping into the bottom of the frame, the fuzzy tassels of the sea oats, threatening to obliterate the view. But I can't help feeling—and I wish I could tell him—that the city is in good hands, and all will be well.

Moon Wind Water Stars

As I look for a way to begin this story, I keep coming back to Iginia. It was she who brought the Huichole Indians into our conversaton that night, high above the town on the windswept ground of the ecology preserve. She was riffing on something Jack had said about a trip he had made to Japan, about the difficulty he had encountered pronouncing Japanese words and phrases. At first I thought she was joking—or was it my poor Spanish?—saying the Huichole Indians speak Japanese. "Of course they don't really speak it," she conceded, seeing my puzzlement. "It just sounds like Japanese, the way they talk." She produced a series of non-sensical syllables in imitation of the Huicholes' Uto-Aztecan language. "Those Huicholes are a little crazy, anyway," she added off-handedly.

We were sitting on straw mats, not far from the blazing *fogata*. When the wind shifted, I tasted the pungent odor of burning mesquite. Along with Iginia, Jack, and myself, there was the impeccably pleasant young woman, Luz.

It was my third visit to San Miguel de Allende. I was studying Spanish at the Instituto, but also seeking new and surer direction for my life. I had been pulled toward Mexico ever since Professor Leon's undergraduate classes in Latin American culture, and since my recent divorce, I had the freedom to pursue my deeper dreams.

I had met Jack only that morning on one of the terraces of

the Posada de las Monjas, where we were both staying. He and his traveling companion, Marianne, had just arrived in San Miguel. I joined them as they finished breakfast, in the simple way strangers fall in with one another in that ancient highland town that encourages everything serendipitous.

As we shared something of our lives, we discovered that we had much in common. Like myself, they had each recently ended marriages that had grown terminally unhappy. Having taken up together, they were now both as delighted as I to be away—even for a spell—from the media, political, and consumerism frenzy that perpetually grips the United States of America. Jack told me that he had lived in Mexico as a boy and was keen to introduce Marianne to a place redolent with happy memories. He then proceeded to bring the great American iconoclast, and literary hero of my youth, Henry Miller, into our conversation. He openly enthused about the freewheeling life Miller pursued as an expatriate in 1930's Paris, and wondered aloud whether "that kind of thing could still happen . . .

"I've thought of chucking my job," he confided, "and taking to the road, maybe settle outside the U.S. for good." He gazed over the terrace wall, toward the hills that rise to the west of town, and seemed to ponder the question. "Maybe once the kids get through school . . ."

While Jack sat silently, lost in some inner calculation, a hummingbird, its feathers shimmering iridiscent in the sunlight, hovered to a potted geranium on the terrace wall and began to feed at its flowers. I looked to Jack—he also turned toward me—and we both laughed. There was no need to voice the allusion that had struck both of us, but we nonetheless did: it was to Miller's famous essay, "Stand Still Like the Hummingbird."

"That's really funny," Jack said. He shifted his hips so that he could reach into his trousers pocket and extract his billfold. "I always carry this card with me, as a sort of inspiration."

He produced a nondescript piece of cardstock from the bill-fold and handed it to me. On it were written, in a precise and steady hand, words I immediately recognized as the most trenchant of Miller's essay. Marianne asked to see it and I gave her the card. Pulling a few strands of hair back from her eyes, she began to read the words aloud: "When you are convinced that all the exits are blocked," she started uncertainly, "either you take to believing in miracles, or you stand still like the hummingbird." She paused a moment, absorbing the words. The Mexican sun shone brightly on her pale skin and yellow hair, and a thin smile formed on her lips. She glanced at the hummingbird, still feeding at the geraniums, before reading on: "The miracle," she pronounced carefully, "is that the honey is always there, right under your nose, only . . . you were too busy searching elsewhere to realize it!" She tossed back her head now and emitted a short, spontaneous laugh. "The worst is not death," she continued, her smile broadening, "but being blind to the fact . . . that everything about life . . . is in the nature of the miraculous!"

I would have been astonished by this uncanny series of coincidences (the affection Jack and I shared for Miller, the card he carrried in his wallet, the hummingbird arriving precisely while we discussed the great writer) but I had come to expect such happenings when I was in San Miguel de Allende. We three sat in the splendid sun of the Mexican altiplano, breathing deeply while we took in Miller's words; all of us, I think, feeling that a bond had been created, a special bond of friendship and fraternity. Jack looked at Marianne and smiled warmly. He reached out his hand. They hadn't been together long, they had explained to me, and their transactions still exuded the fresh feel of a lover's lark. They treated one another with a tentative and tender courtesy.

Marianne hadn't yet said much, so I asked her about her life back in the States. She told me of her daughter, who had just left home. It was a relief to be free of the duties of parenting, she said, but she admitted some anxiety over the thought of her child facing the world's hazards on her own. Then, as if she wanted to move away from stateside thoughts and responsibilities, she dug into her purse and produced a folded newspaper. When she opened it, I saw that it was the official rag of San Miguel's American colony.

"Look at this," she said as she spread the newsprint across the table. "I thought this might be interesting."

In bold letters, taking up a full page of the paper, was an announcement for a celebration at the Charco del Ingenio, the ecology preserve that occupies the high desert east of town. FIRST LUNAR ECLIPSE OF THE MILLENNIUM, that's how it was billed: apparently the expat community had not escaped the American habit of hucksterism. After a brief discussion of the matter, we agreed to meet in the hotel lobby at five. Jack and Marianne went off to their sight-seeing, while I prepared to spend my afternoon working on my Spanish lessons at the municipal library.

That evening we cabbed up the steep, cobbled streets that lead out of town to the east, up to the high ground where the Charco is situated. Though there was still plenty of light, I wished that the sun were yet higher in the January sky: at such times it strikes deep into the walls of the canyon, marking thrilling contrasts with the thick shadows below. I was familiar with the ecology preserve, having made several visits the previous summer; the sun-laden, whispering beauty of the high desert had deeply impressed me. Hoping to have time to explore the terrain before dark, I had urged an early arrival on Marianne and Jack.

And as we ambled along the footpath away from the entrance, with shafts of burnished light spilling through the translucent grasses that undulated among the cactus and mesquite, my new friends seemed as taken by the Charco's peaceful silence as was I. While we walked, Jack told me of his work as a geographer in the American Northwest, building wilderness maps for the Forest Service. I noted admiringly the way he took in our surroundings with an eye trained to observe the land, its structures, and its uses.

He stopped when the canyon came into view. He was particularly intrigued by a defunct aqueduct that runs along the gorge's opposite wall there. Its colossal iron piping is supported by a series of buttresses built into the rock rim, or standing free further toward the town, where the waterworks climbs over a rise before descending onto the spreading plain below. Marianne and I stood with him in awed silence. There was something staggeringly romantic about the structure: visible, from our vantage, at a distance that also suggested temporal displacement toward the simpler, brute era when it was built.

Moving westward, with the sun arcing down across the sky before us, we reached a place where the land drops off in cliffs. From these outcroppings we could see the colonial structures of San Miguel de Allende huddled on the plain below, and then on to the distant ridges west of town. Marianne gazed over the cliffs while Jack and I discussed a catchment basin that lay below.

"We should probably move on," I finally said, "so we don't lose our light."

I led them down the sloping land with an aim to aligning ourselves with the canyon, always moving eastward toward a large reservoir that occupies the other end of the preserve.

Along the way we talked about the different species of cactus we encountered, the alien-looking fruits they bore, and speculated about when they might ripen. We stood stock-still, like amazed children when, just as the sun merged into the western hills in a glowing wash of orange light, the moon rose, large and full, out of the eastern horizon,

Inspired by this singular moment Jack, in his incisive, flinty voice, began to describe the mechanics of the impending eclipse. "The earth," he said, "is always projecting this cone of shadow"—*cone of shadow*, it was this phrase he kept emphasizing—"but this cone of shadow normally just projects itself into the empty void of space. The cone of shadow doesn't hit anything unless the moon moves into its path. Of course, eclipses can only occur at full moons, because of the way things are aligned." He moved his clenched fists in front of his chest, representing the relationship between the earth and the moon.

"You already know about this, of course." He looked me squarely in the eyes. I confessed my tendency, between infrequent episodes of investigation, to allow my knowledge of lunar lore to degenerate into puzzlement. The friendly chuckle that greeted this admission suggested he thought I must be joking. There was a prickly pear cactus nearby. At Marianne's suggestion, we took photos of one another standing in front of it, the ascending moon over our shoulders.

The camera's automatic flash was already operating, and as we moved toward the rim of the canyon, a soft twilight bathed the landscape. When I pointed out a constellation of what I thought were swallows dazzling over the gorge, Marianne, who glanced up briefly without breaking her stride, said simply, "Swifts."

I watched her walk in front of Jack and me. She was a sturdily boned woman, with flaxen hair she wore in bangs. She looked solid and grounded, physical and earthy. Her fair skin was pink from the Mexican sun; she and Jack, she had told me, had spent ten days at Guadalajara before coming to San Miguel. Her native expression seemed to be a contented smile.

She spoke as we walked of how she lived in eastern Oregon, where the land (Jack interjected) bears more affinity to the high country of Idaho than to the temperate rain forests along the coast. She cross-country skied and rode her mountain bike through the wilderness areas near her home. She had the air of a robust Scandinavian; you could see that she was comfortable with nature, and with exerting herself.

She kept up a good pace.

When we reached the canyon, we trod as close to its rim as the contour of the land permitted, occasionally stepping onto a ledge to take a vertiginous look into the darkling gorge. Cactus, brush, and hardy desert trees clung to the canyon wall; in the parched streambed, some sixty yards below, variegated vegetation extracted the water necessary for life. At one of these ledges I pointed out the spot where the previous summer, when I had walked alone through the stilled Charco one late afternoon, I had taken a photograph. The sun had cut deeply into the canyon, and I framed the shot so that my shadow appeared against a nearby boulder, a vertical shape rendered human only by the cheap sombrero that I wore.

Jack pulled up to examine the waterworks at close range. He studied the colossal corroded pipe that ran along the facing canyon wall, and the stone buttresses notched into the cliff some thirty feet below its rim.

"Imagine the effort it took to put that in place," I said, "and with pre-modern technology."

"Yeah," Jack replied, not moving his gaze from the works, "and likely under slave labor conditions. I'll bet they didn't even use safety lines. I imagine more than a few of the—you know, peóns—got killed building that thing."

We stood a moment in silence, as if in commemoration of the arduous lives of those ancient laborers, before we continued eastward towards the reservoir. Several paces on I spotted a large bird flapping away from us, dead up the middle of the canyon. "Hey, look!" I said, "looks like some kind of raptor."

Marianne was nearest me. She didn't respond immediately but glanced toward the bird as she walked on. I could see that she was thinking, taking her time, turning it over in her mind.

"I mean," I went on, "I can't imagine a gull being this far inland; and it was too large for a crow. It didn't look like a buzzard, either."

"Maybe it's a heron," she said suddenly, simply. "Not a great blue, but a simple green heron. Did you notice the way its wings moved? It didn't soar the way a raptor does. It was working too hard."

"Could it be an owl?" I heard myself saying, though I was already succumbing to the feeling that I ought to let her decide the matter. There was something about the way she pondered it, so steadily . . .

"An owl? I don't know." She placed her feet carefully along the stony ground.

"I think you're right," I finally conceded. "It's the way the wings bent, right? A raptor's wings don't bend so hard at the elbow, so to speak."

"That's it!" she said, satisfied with putting it that way. "Maybe we'll get a better look further down the trail."

A couple hundred yards further on, the path began to drop along the canyon wall. We were descending toward a field of broken rock at the base of the dam that holds back the reservoir. The canyon wall crowded up beside us now, with overhanging

vegetation, and the effect was like a grotto. It was very quiet, and the light increasingly dim. There was a sense of moisture, of something rich and fecund, marvelous and hidden.

But, recalling my guidebook's caution against walking in the Charco after dark, on account of some recent muggings, I realized there was also a sense of danger. I didn't say anything, though. What good would it do, except to worry Jack and Marianne?

We caught another glimpse of the mysterious bird as it settled on an outcropping ahead, but there wasn't enough light to make a final judgment from our distance. Continuing our descent along the sheltered path, we eventually came to the base of the dam, right up under the reservoir. Marianne was fascinated by a small stone stucture that sat to one side. It was completely gutted, with nothing but its four outer walls standing; I surmised that it once served as a pump house.

While Jack and I discussed the matter, Marianne went in and climbed the broken steps that jutted from one of its walls. The roof had long ago eroded to time, and when she reached the top, she peered through the last vestiges of twilight down the length of the canyon, oohing and aahing over the view. After she came down, we stepped gingerly through the darkness across boulders that were strewn about the foot of the dam like so much broken crockery. Marianne was disappointed that our bird was no longer in evidence.

We struggled up the embankment alongside the dam until we came level with the surface of the reservoir. The moon had cleared the horizon and now, like a jewel in a violet sky, hung above its opposite shore. I stepped out on the stone paving of the dam to look over the water; Marianne and Jack followed. The lunar disk blazed with a radiance that was inescapable, a whiteness so pure it seemed an invitation to a novel way of seeing things. A strident wind, from which we had been sheltered in the canyon, kicked up the reservoir's surface in insistent, chopping waves. Standing there, I felt the force of these heady powers with an immediacy that was stunning. For a moment I was dumbstruck, unable to move or even think. The water swept violently toward us. Shockingly silver moonlight danced along the skin of the reservoir, its iridescent plaques shifting with the churning mass. The wind blew so rambunctiously I had to brace myself against it.

"Beautiful, isn't it?" Marianne finally said.

Jack and I agreed, and we all turned aside in what I took to be a gesture of self-preservation. Seeking shelter from infinity.

"The stars are certainly bright," I said, breaking the silence that followed. I was accustomed to the sky over my native city, completely washed out by light pollution.

"Yes, even with this bright moon," Jack said, looking up into the heavens. He allowed himself the time to take it all in, slowly, like a connoiseur, before turning to Marianne and me and asking excitedly, "Do you know how to find Polaris?" Receiving no reply, he fixed his gaze again into the sky. "The great thing about Polaris," he went on, his taught voice rising against the raucus wind and waves, "is that no matter where on earth you are—in the northern hemisphere, anyway—you can always orient yourself, if you know how to find that crucial lodestar. Plop me down anywhere," he asserted, "I'm not going to get lost, as long as I can see the sky." He pointed across the canyon. "See that upside-down W up there? That's Cassiopeia. Now, if you sight down from the open end of the W, you'll find Polaris. See, it's simple.

"Do you see it?" he asked Marianne.

She gazed silently into the velvet sky.

"Polaris is positioned between Cassiopeia and the Big

Dipper," Jack explained further, not waiting for a reply. "We can't see the Dipper at the moment, though, because it's still below the horizon . . ."

Marianne and I stood gaping in wonderment.

"Watch this," Jack suddenly erupted, bracing up his torso in an exaggerated manner. "If we begin to walk toward Polaris, we'll be traveling due north." He had turned toward one end of the dam; and he now shuffled in place in a clowning, Michael Jackson moonwalk, all the while looking vaguely towards the North Star. Marianne and I lined up behind him and mimicked our own shuffle. We were following him across the planet, trekking into the night. "As we walk," Jack called out behind him, "we'll always keep Polaris to our north; though as we travel along, it will rise ever further above the horizon. Do you see? Then, when we finally reach the North Pole, it will be directly overhead!"

He turned to Marianne and I. We were all drunk with the earth and laughing, as if we could really walk to the North Pole; so exhilarating it was to be on the high plateau, absorbed in the night sky . . .

We left the dam and started up a path to the preserve entrance. Midway there Marianne backtracked to relieve herself. While Jack and I chatted, waiting for her, I heard a little yelp from the direction she had taken. I turned around instinctively, the guidebook's warning of muggings somewhere in the back of my mind. There, a hundred feet down the path, Marianne's bare bottom shone opalescent in the silver moonlight. I quickly turned to Jack, not wanting him to think I would sneak a glimpse of his woman half-naked.

Marianne returned. To erase any suspicion—suspicion, that is, that I had looked toward Marianne in hopes of catching her in a state of undress—I said, "I thought I heard you calling out down there." She responded, a little sheepishly, I thought, "Yeah, I guess I did sing a little something." Then after a pause, as if to gauge how that went over, she added, "When I pee outside I like to make, well, a sort of ritual out of it, like an animal marking its territory or something. That way, if a male comes along, he'll know that I've been there."

I thought of the muggers. "I don't know if that would be so good," I said. "Jack and I would have to defend your honor. And I can't speak for Jack, but I'm no prizefighter."

"That's okay," she said with a smile, "Jack's a champion sumo wrestler."

Jack flexed his muscles. "That's right," he said, "I weigh three hundred pounds."

Jack is incredibly skinny.

"You must be very dense," I said.

"I am," he laughed.

Marianne sighed and we continued our trek toward the higher ground at the Charco entrance. When we arrived there we milled through the crowd that had gathered near a seething bonfire—the *fogata*—that the Charco staff had built.

Jack's delight in reviving his acquaintance with the Mexicans—and in using his still functional Spanish—was palpable. We took up separate positions around the fire, each of us seeking warmth, but also to avoid the richly acrid smoke that shifted with the insistent wind that scoured the bare, high desert country. Marianne sat against the large stones that ringed the fire-pit while Jack wandered off to a table where ladies served punch and mezcal.

When I went to find him he had struck up a conversation with Iginia and Luz. They were sitting on one of the wide, plaited mats the Charco staff had laid around the fire in concentric rings. They were drinking punch: it was only later that Jack began with the mezcal, making trips to the fire to supply Marianne with the small ceramic cups sold at five pesos a shot.

After the bit about the Huicholes speaking Japanese, Iginia continued in a more serious vein, with a tone of awe, if not reverence. "They go on their peyote journeys every year," she said. "They go to a place three hundred kilometers north of here. And when they ingest the peyote, they have visions." She emphatically widened her eyes, as if to make sure that we understood. Luz sat attentively, content. "Whatever they see in those visions will guide them all year long, until the next pilgrimage. Whatever it is, no matter how crazy it might be, they have to do it. Because Peyote tells them to!"

Her expression turned to one of honest disbelief. She got up and went to buy tamales.

The crowd had grown considerably and people were still arriving. The light of the bonfire did not stretch far into the deepening darkness, and I sensed the milling throng more than saw them. It was nonetheless good to be in the midst of that gathering, whose voices were percolating around and above us. It was just before eight; the moon had yet to move into the earth's shadow. It was some thirty degrees over the horizon, still full and very bright.

Iginia came back with tamales for all of us, red and green. I sat cross-legged on the mat, facing the woman named Luz. I was vaguely curious about how Jack had fallen in with these two women but did not ask. Nor did it seem that Luz and Iginia had been acquainted prior to our chance gathering.

Iginia was a mature and apparently sophisticated woman. She communicated directly and forcefully, with a touch of irony, and seemed to know a great deal about what went on in the world. Luz was different. Her mannerisms bespoke a humble—and no doubt local—upbringing. She sat simply, waiting for nothing in particular; spoke little, but evinced no discomfort among three older strangers so different from her in background. I was struck by the sense of humble ease she exuded.

Her braided hair encircled her head like a tiara.

She inquired into my life and purposes in her town, and I learned something of her. She was patient with my poor Spanish, exerting herself to understand without stopping to correct my errors.

"I'm studying to be a teacher," she told me enthusiastically.

"Which grades?" I asked.

"Elementary."

She paused and cast down her eyes. "But I wasn't studying the entire time," she added. "I stopped for a while."

Her pained expression gave out that her reasons for stopping were not ones she considered worthy.

"I'm not going to stop now," she resolutely concluded, peering straight ahead into the night.

"I'll bet you won't," I said, and I meant it. Though her demeanor was as mild as the madonna, I sensed, within her, some core capable of undying resistance.

She sat rocking on her haunches and gently nodded her head.

We were waiting for the moon, for Jack's cone of shadow to engulf it in darkness. I occasionally checked the watch I had bought prior to the trip. It was a Timex with the legacy company's trademarked *Indiglo*.

"What I like most about this watch," I told Luz, "is the light. See, isn't it beautiful?"

"Yes, it is."

I confessed that I sometimes found myself checking the time just to see that gorgeous greenish glow.

"Mine doesn't have a light." She held out her wrist. "It

doesn't have anything. It's just a watch."

We fell silent, struck by the mysteries of time, or perhaps only by the gulf in timepiece selection available to middle class Americans and working class Mexicans.

Suddenly Luz looked up and blurted, "I think it's starting. Look!"

Indeed, one edge of the moon was beginning to go murky. Enlivened by the event the four of us, as darkness invested the beleaguered sphere, chatted together excitedly. From time to time Luz referred to the progress of the eclipse, and she would encourage me to take a look. "Yes," I replied on one of these occasions, "it looks like someone took a bite . . . alguien está comiendo la luna."

We stayed there together like that for some time, content in one another's company, until the moon was nothing but a dusky shadow. But it was getting colder and colder on the exposed ground with the wind, real cold, and I finally grew tired of sitting immobile, defenseless against the elements. I went to the fire, where I explored various strategies to avoid the choking fumes that ambushed you when the wind shifted. After thawing some, I left the fogata and wandered through the crowd. People sat on the ground in small circles, enjoying private picnics with candles in glass jars, a low radio, or murmured conversations. One group of drunken Americans was having a good time. "Someone must have forgotten to pay the moon bill!" one of them kept bellowing.

Finally, feeling I had had as much of THE FIRST ECLIPSE OF THE MILLENNIUM as I had bargained for, I went to tell Jack and Marianne that I was returning to the posada. They were standing near the fire, talking with Iginia. Luz wasn't around, and no one knew where she had gone. Jack and Marianne decided to leave with me—"We came together, we'll leave together," Marianne said—so we said goodbye to Iginia, walked to the entrance, and radioed to town for a cab.

On leaving the Instituto the next morning I was surprised by brass bands and fireworks in the street. School children in blue and white uniforms sat on the curbs all along the Ancho de San Antonio. A parade was beginning. It was the birthday of Ignacio Allende, hero of Mexican independence and namesake of the town. I rushed to the posada to collect Jack and Marianne; we walked up Canal and arrived at the Escuela de Bellas Artes as the front of the parade rounded the corner.

Drums kept up a loud, steady beat as, one by one, the students of the town's myriad primary schools ("the demographic profile," Jack explained) filed by. At the front of each group was a select cadre who carried the school's banner. Each school had a distinctive uniform and colors. Many were accompanied by a small brass band, or a drum and bugle corps. As each squadron reached the corner, one of the students would bark an instruction and the file would turn, sharply or desultorily, and move away past Bellas Artes.

The schools came on one after another: the incessant, simple drumbeats, squadron leaders calling out the turns, bright colors of the banners and uniforms, the burnished complexions of the children, their expressions happy, bored, or vague, and all of them moving, everything movement now and excitement, color, and sound! I felt we were watching the future of Mexico streaming by and said so to Jack; he grinned and nodded. Later came the secondary schools, the equestrian guard, and finally the tanks—the business end of the *República*. Clouds of gaily colored helium balloons sought out the bright sky; they floated lazily away as the noise of the parade dissipated into the northern reaches of the town.

After lunch I showed Marianne and Jack the artisan market,

where they bought gifts for their children back in the States. Later that evening we attended a concert of flamenco music in the town's small theatre; afterward we went across to Tio Lucas's place to dine. We talked about synchronicity and ultimate meanings, but also about Montezuma's revenge and working for a living. It was past midnight when we returned to the posada. As they were leaving in the morning, we said our goodbyes. I returned to my room and sat on the edge of my simple bed, satiated both with Mexico and their friendship.

In the morning I told Maria Elena—my Spanish teacher—about the eclipse party. I confided that I regretted not having said goodbye to Luz. I was cold and tired; and the truth is, I hadn't made an effort to locate her. The simple, calm way she sat with us, encouraging my inexpert attempts at communication, sharing something of her own story, keeping me informed of the progress of the eclipse, left me with a sentimental debt: one that at the least required, I felt, a decent farewell. Looking back that next day, I saw her as an unobtrusive and yet masterful facilitator, welcoming me in some inconceivable way to a richer experience not only of her people's culture, but to the earth. To life itself. Sitting by that blazing fire, thousands of miles from my native city, I had felt truly at home.

That afternoon I found it impossible to follow my normal routine, translating poems and stories at the library. Instead I wandered far into the northern outskirts of the town. The idea was a bit whimsical, but with few restraints on my time, I could afford to indulge it. Luz had told me that she worked in a bakery. She had also mentioned the name of the street, but I had forgotten it. I was certain it wasn't in the Centro, at least; I knew the streets around the plaza like the back of my hand and would have remembered the name. That meant that it had to be located in one of the outlying neighborhoods.

In sum, I spent the afternoon describing a wide, walking arc across the northern side of San Miguel de Allende. It wasn't a determined effort to find the bakery, but I was keeping my eyes open. I entered one large establishment, with brick interior walls, the aroma of loaves baking in ovens and, on metal racks around its periphery, sweet pastries. The door to the back shop being ajar, I peered in for a look at the workforce. Two young men clowned near one of the large ovens; they were alone. I saw a good many other interesting things on my walk, but no sign of Luz. Finally tiring of the sun and exertion, I returned to my room. "I could do the south side tomorrow," I told myself, "and still have next week for the east and west quadrants . . ."

Don't mistake me. I wasn't in love, unless it was with the earth, with the sky, with an entire people. But something had happened with Luz, and I felt I had to make some gesture, something to express the simple connection we had made. I thought of different routes I could take around the town and its outskirts, all the while recognizing that the odds of finding her were slim. The fact is, I wasn't sure she had said "bakery." It might have been "pastry shop," which in Mexico is something different. And if she worked in a shop's back workroom, or even worse, in a wholesale bakery, my chances of seeing her from the street side of things were negligible.

The next day I followed my standard routines. Too tired for further wanderings in the altiplano sun, I accepted the fact that the idea of finding Luz was a pipe dream.

But midway through the afternoon, while painstakingly working my way, in the library's reference room, through one of Julio Cortázar's short stories, I was distracted by movement on the edge of my field of vision. And when I glanced away from the page, I noted a familiar form, her golden-brown hair encircling her head like a tiara, walking away from the pencil sharpener and out of the room. I got up and followed across the hall to where the short and softly rounded young woman seemed to have gone. To my surprised delight, in another room, seated at one of the dark, heavy tables, was Luz. She seemed happy to see me. She told me that she was studying for an exam; a text on ecology lay open before her.

She invited me to sit down.

"I'm not working at the bakery anymore," she said excitedly. "I got a new job, working on the Census."

"You'll be interviewing people," I said. "That's great, you'll learn a lot about your country. It will make you a better teacher."

"Yes," she said cheerfully.

We didn't have a great deal more to say to one another, and after a few casual remarks I began to feel out of place. I suggested that I let her get back to her studying, and we agreed to exchange addresses.

"Do you have e-mail?" I asked as she wrote in my notebook.

She passed the notebook back to me. She had limned her street address in pink felt pen, in a hand regular and vertical. Nice school teacher block letters.

"Just that," she said, apologetically, "no telephone or anything."

I admired her courage, struggling against material limitations that would stop us Americans dead in our tracks.

"Don't give up," I finally said.

"I won't."

I felt more settled, leaving Luz there studying, knowing about her new job with the Census. It seemed certain that she would prevail, be a vital part of the future along with all those children in the parade: guiding them, teaching them. In nice but halting English she said, as I passed through the door, "Have a nice trip."

A lot can happen in a day or two. I've found myself thinking a great deal about my meetings with Jack and Marianne, Iginia and Luz, about the evening of the eclipse celebration, and the convergence of raw energies I felt so powerfully on the dam by the reservoir. Iginia's story of the Huichole Indians came to mind, and I could believe that that moment by the water, with the wind and the moon, along with the entire ambit of events and encounters that surrounded it, had been a vision: a vision that, like those of the Huicholes, could surely guide me for a year or even longer. I had been taught to watch birds more carefully, instructed in the stars, warmed by a fire built by anonymous others, given food prepared by strangers, welcomed in the most simple way into another people's culture; and I had seen that *cone of shadow* fall across the face of the moon. Just as Miller had written in his famous essay, the world is a place of extravagant bounty—of marvels and wonders—there for the taking, if only we give ourselves permission to explore, and be willing to open our eyes!

Wandering near the Instituto one day, not long after the eclipse celebration, I came across some terra cotta masks in a ceramics workshop. On each was represented the sun and a half-moon in several designs. I chose two among those I thought the finest and hand-carried them through the flight home. I sent them to Jack and Marianne the other day. I am now on the lookout for a watch: a ladies watch with a lighted dial. If on its face it bears a fancifully depicted moon, so much the better . . .

The Snow Geese

I WAS WITH MY FATHER. We were driving to Maryland's Eastern Shore, from where we both live in the Washington suburbs. Winter was coming on as we sped under a sky like goose down, crossing the mighty bridge over the Chesapeake, and then cruising past ancient hamlets and slumbering fields. We were heading toward Salisbury, two and a half hours distant, where I had a couple hours work with a client. It was a long drive I had accomplished too many times on my own, so quite aside from the benefit of providing an outing for my retired parent, I was grateful for the company. I had sweetened the offer with a promise to visit the Blackwater Wildlife Refuge, a vast expanse of marshland, and one of the East Coast's major stopping places for migratory waterfowl. No stranger to the preserve, I told the old man that on this cloudy December day there would be an excellent chance of seeing large numbers of wintering geese and swans in the marshes.

My father had retired a couple years earlier from the wholesale groceries trade. He started life behind the eight ball, having grown up in searing rural poverty in southern Maryland's deep countryside. With an indomitable will he cleared a path for himself that brought him to retirement as the major partner in a concern that employed some fifty people. In the process, he also created the haven where my sister and brother and I grew to maturity.

At his retirement dinner I was moved by the affection evinced toward him by his employees, as well as his partners and customers. He had always been a man's man, and it was easy to understand the camaraderie he enjoyed with pals with whom he'd played countless rounds of golf, bet on football games, visited the track, or sat up late on Saturday nights playing poker and drinking beer. I knew without thinking about it that they appreciated, as did I, his ready sense of humor and penchant for telling colorful stories.

What came as more of a surprise were the powerful connections he had forged with the firm's rank and file employees, especially the women who made up the company's administrative staff. I'm sure his good looks and gallant attitude toward the opposite sex didn't hurt his chances of winning their favor; nor could they have been insensitive to the policy he pioneered whereby no one in the firm, including the partners themselves, could earn more than four times the salary of the concern's lowest paid employee. But there was something in their heartfelt expressions of sorrow over his departure, many telling me they would miss him with tears in their eyes, that went beyond appreciation for his masculine qualities, or any brute calculation of benefits accrued through their mutual business dealings. Perhaps it had to do, I surmised, with an ingrained sense of honor, a determination to do the right thing that I had come, throughout my childhood, to appreciate as one of my father's salient characteristics.

I tried to convey something of this in the testimonial I had been asked to deliver that night. I related how I had gone one day, when I was ten years old, to the open field that abutted our suburban housing tract to collect dirt for potting an African violet I had acquired somewhere. When my father discovered me coming into the yard with the bucketful of soil, he asked where

I had gotten it, and I told him. "Take it back," he instructed me. "Why?" I asked. "It's not ours," he said. "It belongs to the people who own the field." "It's only some dirt," I rejoined. "They wouldn't care." "Did you ask them?" he said. "No." "Well, if you ask them, and they say it's all right, you can keep it."

I reluctantly returned the soil to the field, not wishing to tromp to the farmhouse at the end of the dirt road and confront the grouchy man who lived there with a request for some of his real estate.

In the days that followed the banquet I was beset by nagging misgivings about my filial tribute. In particular, my inclusion of the dirt anecdote troubled me. I had meant the episode to reflect positively on the old man's sense of honor; but in hindsight it struck me that his reaction to my act of petty larceny may have been judged excessively strict—even fanatical—by some of my auditors. I hadn't thought to explain, I regretted, that having lived and worked on farms as a boy, my father no doubt possessed a greater sense of the value of soil than those with less intimacy with the earth. Nor did I point out that the grouchy man at the end of the dirt road was in the habit of complaining to neighborhood parents about kids trespassing on his property, complaints the old man judiciously overlooked in the face of his sons' natural desire to explore the woods and fields that surrounded our dwelling in the far suburbs.

I cheered myself with the thought that the more astute of my auditors no doubt understood one simple fact: my father's response was an object lesson. It wasn't about the bucket of dirt, but about teaching me to respect the rights of others. Years later, when I was in college, I was out shopping with a girlfriend and her father. The father, let's just call him Mr. Jones, was fiddling with some gadget he needed for the house. In the course of his fiddling, turning the device this way and that, forcefully twisting one part and another, the product snapped. He laid it back on the shelf, said "Oh, well," and we departed the store in a respectable hurry. I was shocked, knowing that if the old man had committed a similar error, he would have taken the merchandise to the counter and offered to pay for it.

It was then that I began to be grateful for his demanding ethical rules.

Yet still there was something about my tribute speech that left me unsettled, a dissatisfaction I had not yet managed to resolve as my father and I made our way past field and forest, creek and cove on that cloudy December day. He had come across the dais at my speech's conclusion, tears in his eyes and, wrapping me in one of his famous bear hugs, said, "That was the nicest thing anyone has ever said to me." But given the several cocktails he had put away—he no more comfortable in the limelight than I had been giving the speech—I suspected his reaction would have been similar had I taken to the podium and sang the Battle Hymn of the Republic. As much as it pained me, I remained convinced that my tribute had failed to capture the essence of the old man's character. Though I could not put my finger on it, I knew there was something vital I had left out, something to explain the tears in his employees' eyes at the prospect of his departure.

As we cruised along the highway to Salisbury, surrounded on every side by the beauty of Maryland's Eastern Shore—croplands spreading across the flat earth to distant stands of forest, coves and creeks and little towns, and Canada geese scavenging in the fields—we spoke of many things. Now that he had retired, the old man's days were filled with monitoring the market, where his retirement funds were invested, helping my kid sister Pooky with her toddlers, and following the news on television. He had many ideas about how to fix the nation's woes, and he was not shy about sharing them. The spate of wrongdoing by business leaders then coming to light was deplorable, he said, and in spite of a conservative orientation natural in a man whose life story signaled the power of free enterprise as a vehicle of self-transformation, he thought CEOs and boards of directors should be made more responsive to shareholders—even if it took stern measures by their regulators. He also felt passionately, he told me, that the country ought to afford healthcare for everyone, regardless of their economic status. "There are some things that just shouldn't be part of the marketplace," he said. "We're talking about life and death. A person can't help it if they're sick."

"Heck, Dad," I couldn't help gently ribbing him, "if I didn't know better, I'd say you were in danger of becoming one of us liberals."

"No," he insisted, "it's just a matter of human decency."

We drove on, chatting about these kinds of things, and then he shared several anecdotes about the grandchildren he loved and doted upon. As he described taking my small nephew Andrew to the local swim center, I was gobsmacked by a memory from my own childhood:

It is a bright summer weekend, of the kind on which my parents regularly take us to one of the wading beaches along the Chesapeake—a poor man's holiday for Washington's working classes. There is a small amusement park there and also a large swimming pool. I love being in the water, but not yet having learned to swim, and terrified of drowning, I confine my aquatic adventures to clinging desperately to the pool's edge. Seeing my predicament, my father holds out his arms like a tray. I lie across them on my stomach. As he walks about in the shallow end, I practice kicking my feet and moving my arms. I feel an untrammeled glee, never worried for a moment that I will come to harm while he is there.

We soon reached Salisbury, and I dropped the old man at the local mall, where he would occupy himself while I dealt with my clients, one of the big poultry concerns on the Shore. I returned to the mall when I finished; we had a bite to eat at the food court.

Our route to the refuge took us off the main highway onto narrow asphalt roads that wound through woods of loblolly pines. Loblollies are also a hallmark species of the part of the state where my father came up and, growing nostaligic, he began to reminisce about his childhood in the countryside. "I used to go through the woods after school," he said. "I'd collect the needles of those loblolly pines in a wheelbarrow. Of course we couldn't afford straw for the animals' bedding . . ."

Of course. Bought straw was in the same unattainable category as other luxuries for my father's Depression-era, rural family, luxuries like running water, electricity—and regular meals.

A little further on a band of crows flew across the road. "You know," my father said, seemingly out of nowhere, "a lot of people don't realize it, but those crows are beautiful birds."

It seemed an odd remark: crows had always struck me as quintessentially ordinary, and their incessant cawing outside my apartment window, when I sat trying to concentrate at my desk, annoying. There was an awkward silence and then, with a distinct hesitation in his voice, my father gazed out the window and again began to speak, plunged anew into memories of distant childhood . . .

"When I was about ten or eleven," he said, "I was learning to use this .22 caliber rifle we had at the house. One day I took it out into the woods sand, after wandering around awhile, found this crow sitting up in a tree. I leveled the gun, got the bird in

my sights, and pulled the trigger. Well, that crow dropped right to the ground, and boy was I proud of myself! A direct hit! I ran over to where the bird had fallen, so I could take a closer look, and when I got to it, taking hold of one of its wings, I stretched it out. Now, I'd always thought, like a lot of people I guess, that crows are just black. But underneath that wing, there were all these different colors. Hues of purple, green, blue, gold . . . and they all had this beautiful sheen! Anyway, kneeling there like that, I got a sickening feeling deep in my gut. I guess I couldn't believe I had killed something so beautiful. In any case, I decided right there and then that I would never again kill a living creature, at least not unless it was under the most urgent necessity."

The old man's tale left a somber residue—one tinged with remorse—and we covered the remaining ground to the refuge in silence. From time to time we passed other crows along the road, or trucking across the open sky above, squawking loudly in what it was hard not to imagine were recriminatory tones. My father appeared lost in the depths of his being; I wondered if he too feared something accusatory in their presence, a wrong still unexpiated. At last, crossing a low bridge, we entered the wildlife preserve.

We walked a pine-shaded trail to open water, a great, still expanse of silvered blue which, though beautiful in the muted light, was devoid of the transient waterfowl we sought. After admiring the view for several minutes, we trekked back to the car and drove to an area of the preserve where I believed, based on previous visits, our chances of sighting migratory flocks were promising. We parked at a small parking pad and set out on foot along the loop route that runs through the marshes. Well along the road, surrounded by marsh-grass-studded water stretching as far as we could see, we spotted the snow geese. The flocks comprised several thousand birds, I estimated, but they were not close enough, even with our binoculars, to get a good look. I judged them to be several hundred yards distant.

We stood and waited for some time, hoping the birds might move closer, but they exibited no intention of shifting their position. The National Geographic moment I had all but promised my father was tantalizingly close but unachieved, the geese no more than blurry specks of white against the greenish dun of the marsh's further reaches.

The afternoon was fast declining, and the cold December wind increasingly penetrated our clothing. Finally the old man, his neck hunched into the upturned collar of the light fall jacket he wore, suggested we leave; without waiting for my response, he began to walk toward the car. The aging, underdressed man had clearly had his fill of viewing indeterminate specks in the distance. In spite of my disappointment (we had come so close!) I followed behind.

We had gone no more than ten paces, however, when I heard a distinctive sound behind us: the hollow, percussive draft of thousands upon thousands of beating wings.

We both turned to look.

The entire flock of distant snow geese, en masse, had lifted off the marsh. It was one of the most mesmerizing things I had ever witnessed. They rose in a slow vortex, a continually rising spiral that expanded in a precise chaos of honking and flapping, rising and spreading until their scattered forms nearly obliterated the horizon. Then, something even more astonishing happened. The entire body of birds, still weaving and shuttling in a spinning galaxy of white, began to move towards my father and me. Through some collective intelligence too mind-boggling to fathom, the flock displaced itself laterally through the air while continuing to churn in its vortex, moving ever closer, until they were directly in front of us. It was thrilling beyond measure. Finally, reversing the process by which they had lifted off, the geese slowly settled into the marsh again, revolving and lowering, right before our eyes!

I felt gratified that the old man had gotten the chance to see the migratory flocks I had promised when I invited him to share my drive to the Shore. After admiring the birds for some time, we returned to the car and set out for home. Our spirits were light as we spoke of many things, but chiefly how my kid sister was faring as a new mother, and also about the characteristics of the two toddlers my father spent so much time looking after since his retirement.

Later, as we circled Washington on its beltway, closing on home in silence now, I understood that the old man's gratuitous shooting of the crow, while still a boy, had long been expiated: this, to me, was the meaning of the stupendous gesture of the snow geese, a gesture which incontrovertibly welcomed our presence in their domain of teeming life. For weren't the geese confirming, in a fashion too magnificent to ignore, that he had long since learned the lesson of that fateful outing in the woods? That lesson, after all, was about caring for life, and my father had devoted his to caring first for his children, then his employees, and now his grandchildren. As for me, I had found the key to my dissatisfaction with my retirement-dinner tribute. Having emphasized the old man's companionableness, his forthrightness, his strength of will and even the probity of his character, I had omitted what was probably the most important feature of his personality: a deep penchant for taking care of those around him.

I dropped him at his townhouse with the usual goodbyes and drove home in awed silence, amazed by the things you can learn on a simple December day.

I Wanna Hear It Again

What your heart thinks great, is great.
>   —Emerson, "Spiritual Laws"

ALTHOUGH PENNSYLVANIA AVENUE is among the world's more famous streets, only one of the capital's long-time denizens will tell you that, from the celebrated residence at 1600, the avenue staggers brokenly toward the legislative branch, leaps diagonally over the Capitol, and for some dozen blocks assumes the genteel character of a southern boulevard before bridging over the sluggish green Anacostia. Once over the river, the avenue climbs abruptly for a half-mile to a leafy summit from which it descends gently into the Maryland suburbs' more open vistas; finally free of the city's gravity, L'Enfant's ceremonial passage metamorphoses into a galloping highway which, after bisecting the bedroom community of District Heights, plunges headlong towards the Prince George's County bottomlands where tobacco once reigned as God Supreme. At Upper Marlboro—where in 1812 Commodore Barney torched his riverboats to keep them out of the hands of advancing British troops—the thoroughfare marks sharply southward through farm and forest, ending only when it reaches the tip of the peninsula where the Patuxent pours into the Chesapeake at Solomon's Island.

It was somewhere less than midway along this course from world capital to tidewater fishing village that the events related here took place. As the Kennedy administration settled into the White House, developers were putting down subdivisions in the lee of Andrews Air Base, ten or fifteen miles southeast of Washington. The houses they built sheltered the families of men stationed at the base (a sprawling city unto itself) along with those of the growing legion of civil servants, as well as members of myriad private occupations, who supported the peculiar economy of the nearby capital.

One of these subdivisions carried the heraldic moniker "Kingston Manor." The *Manor* consisted of two streets, running at right angles, lined with two and three bedroom ramblers priced to suit the budgets of the struggling young families who bought into the neighborhood. To the south and east spread fields planted in corn and tobacco. On the north, beyond a narrow belt of forest, another newly-minted housing development catered to a better-heeled market: Air Force officers and senior civil servants. To the west was a reach of low ground the neighborhood kids called the swamp; beyond its soggy acres lay the colossal primitiveness of the gravel pit. Just past the pit's far edge, where a narrow footpath skirted its radically sloping walls, a chain-link fence announced the inviolable border of the air base.

It was amid these varied landscapes that Moose—whose moniker derived not from his build, which was far from robust, but from an almost totemic attachment to a well-known cartoon character—did the greater part of his growing up. His family moved to Kingston Manor when he was six years old; until then they had lived right on the city's border in Capitol Heights. *The Heights*, as his mother referred to the place, was developed as a cottage community in the early years of the century. She had grown up there, and she regularly drove her boys back to the old neighborhood to visit Moose's grandmother in the cramped bungalow his grandfather, Gus, built along one of its shady, sloping streets in the nineteen-twenties. Sometimes, after visiting with Moose's grandmother, they would stroll along an adjoining lane to drop in on Moose's great grandmother, who carried on alone in the white clapboard house, with its decommissioned outhouse in back and coal-fueled cooking stove, where his grandmother was raised. When time allowed, a further amble up and down the Heights' many declivities brought them to assorted uncles and aunts, great and otherwise, and cousins removed by varying degrees.

Moose's grandfather had died two years before Moose was born, but his presence in the bungalow was palpable. Banjo on knee, he was the man in the striped jacket and straw hat (the outfit of the ragtime band in which he moonlighted and which, along with Moose's grandmother, was his passion in life) staring jauntily out from the framed photograph on a side table near the television set. Descending into the bungalow's dark, dank cellar, Moose and his brothers would quizzically examine the paraphernalia of the painting contracting business that was Gus's day job, and the main source of security for his family: half-empty paint cans, stiff brushes and bushy rollers, broad dropcloths of heavy canvas. Later they would climb into Gus's old fishing skiff, which still occupied the garage under the summer room, and pretend they were JFK and the crew of PT-109, scouring Pacific waters for Japanese Imperial Navy vessels.

The *Heights*, all this is to say, was a place saturated with Moose's mother and her kin. As such, the move to the Manor represented a rectification towards a paternal influence, his father having come up amid the dirt farm poverty of southern Maryland corn and tobacco.

The displacement countryward did no harm to Moose. He thrived among the forests and fields, the swamp and the gravel pit. His family's house was situated at the end of the Manor's main street; beyond the house a dirt and gravel drive ran past the swamp to a big, white farmhouse. The farmhouse and its entire end of the dirt road were off-limits to Moose and his brothers; it was all private property, and the owner had let it be known that he would not countenance trespassing by neighborhood ragamuffins. Nonetheless the boys often caught stray glimpses of the imposing structure while tromping through the woods on vital military expeditions against Wermacht strongholds.

Moose and his brothers were accompanied in their adventures by a half-wild mongrel dog their father bought for them the summer they moved to the Manor. The dog grew up with them, and they with him, and he became one of them.

The landscapes that surrounded the neighborhood teemed with yet wilder things. The swamp was full of bullfrogs in summer, fat sleek ones the boys of the neighborhood stalked and captured; every spring, the murky waters where the creek spread over the low ground pullulated with tadpoles. Throughout quiet June nights, the shrill cries of spring peepers could be heard in chorus with the crickets in the lawns and woods. Toads were always turning up under splashblocks, and Ricky next door, Moose's friend, had a knack for capturing leathery-skinned rat snakes. He kept them in aquarium tanks in the basement until they escaped and roamed the house, perhaps roam still. In autumn, crows flocked by the thousands in the trees that lined the old farm road. Then Moose would stand under the leaden sky, listening to their portentous crawing, and wonder where they would all go.

During the spring and summer of Moose's ninth year, a series of events occurred that wrenched his life irretrievably from its previous moorings. The opening wedge in this metamorphosis came just as winter started to break, when one of the Hinneman's German Shepherds gave birth. Every evening after dinner Moose would cross the street and sit by the litter in the warmly humid basement, fascinated by the rubbery softness of the puppies' bodies, their awkward helplessness; by the odor of new flesh and mother's milk; and by the big furry bitch's supine protectiveness.

Then, as the season swelled toward summer, there were the mice at the Beall's. The Bealls lived at the front of the neighborhood, near the county road. The father was an electrician and there were three sons in the elementary school. And all of the family's males possessed the same unusual pigmentation, pale pinkish skin with irregular reddish blotches on and around the scalp. Moose happened to be at their house, that day in late spring, when Mr. Beall discovered the infestation. He brought the newly born mice into the back yard and placed them on a pyre of kindling and newspaper. With the clarity of a child's vision, Moose noted every detail of the pathetically small creatures: the pressed blindness of their closed eyes, the curled feet, the fresh piglet pinkness that conjured an eerie resonance with the coloring of the Bealls themselves. He watched the neighborhood men and older boys go about their task with a voluble alacrity; and when they doused the miniature pyre with gasoline, and invited the holocaust with a tossed match, he smelled the sickly stench of burning flesh . . .

The *pièce de résistance* of this cluster of startling events came in the heart of summer, when little Joey, the Hinneman's six-year-old, died. The family had been visiting with friends over the Fourth of July weekend, their car parked on a sloping drive; Joey got behind the wheel when no one was looking and managed to shift the transmission into neutral. When the car began to roll, he panicked and jumped out. Falling under the wheels, he was killed. Things were very quiet at the end of Rosemont Street that midsummer, and the Hinnemans gave antiqued gold statuettes to their friends and neighbors as a remembrance. A pair of these appeared one day on the mantel above the fireplace in Moose's living room. One depicted a faunish boy in peasant rags playing the flute, his eyes fixed obliquely upward. His peasant-girl companion, on the other side of the mantel, held her ears. Her anguished expression told Moose that, try as she might, she could not block out her mate's shrill and discordant death-dirge.

These mysteries of birth, death, and life's mudane cruelties set Moose to questioning a world he had, up until then, accepted at face value. He began to confront a growing realization that things didn't seem right around his family home, and also in other areas of his life. His mother, normally nurturing and cheerful, periodically erupted in bursts of manic anger, particularly when she was trapped at the desolate rambler with her unruly sons through the endless days of summer vacation. One day she violently slung a glass ashtray across the living room, narrowly missing Moose's younger brother, Tad. There was also Moose's father. Did he have to, Moose wondered, order everyone around in that gruff manner? And the way he sometimes treated Moose's mother was clearly insensitive, even to a nine-year-old. Returning home from work one day, he brusquely stated that the drapes she had spent all week laboring over looked "stupid," reducing her to helpless tears. As for the teachers at school, why were they so downright mean? Moose didn't relish seeing Mrs. Mehan again, who in the spring had grabbed him on the playground, just because he had gotten a little exuberant on the slide, and nearly shook the life out of him.

By August Moose grew more quiet than was usual. He took to observing the sky a great deal, even when it was not ringing with the calls of crows. The towering cumuli that drifted over the neighborhood, trailing cool shadows across lawns and streets, held him rapt for what seemed endless moments; he studied the ridged and rippled patterns of the cirri that at times fixed themselves in the remote blueness of those bright afternoons like his life depended on it. When smoky black thunderheads flowed out of the countryside to the south, he was unable to utter a sound, but stood spellbound as the mongrel dog raced in berserk circles through the charged air.

Moose might have remained forever fixed in this silent watchfulness had it not been for the Piano Man. Walter Mecklin made his appearance late in August, shortly before Moose and his brothers, along with the rest of the neighborhood children, returned to school.

It was a hot Saturday afternoon when Walter pulled up with Audrey and the kids in the big, angular Plymouth. After the doors unfolded slowly into the placid brightness, Walter emerged first, his awkward frame appearing over the roof of the car as he rose into the sunlight. He faltered as he sidestepped the phlox Moose's father had planted along the driveway, but then regained his balance in an operation that depended upon some impossible coordination between his ungainly limbs. Meanwhile Audrey emerged from the passenger door. Her hair was what Moose noticed first: gently waved, and of a grayish taupe he had never seen before. She was nearly as tall as Walter, at least six feet, with broad, boxy hips; her subtly labored manner of walking suggested difficulty in moving her long legs. The movements of her shoulders, however, and of her expressive eyes and mouth, were not without grace.

Moose's mother came to the front door and, at the sight of Audrey, rushed down the steps of the concrete porch and over to the drive, where she buried herself in the larger woman's enfolding embrace. The two women stepped back and, holding hands, looked into one another's faces in shocked amazement.

"Gosh Maug, how the heck have you been?" They were stepping up to the walk.

"I'm fine as ever. These are my boys."

Moose and his brothers stood lined up along the walk, waiting for something to happen.

"Hi boys," Audrey said in her husky, drawled voice, bending her towering form towards them.

They politely said hello, as they had been taught to do with new acquaintances.

"Do you know who I am?"

The boys fidgeted their sneakers across the rough concrete.

"Come on boys," Moose's mother said. "I told you about the Mecklins."

"Weren't you my mother's friend?" Moose's older brother, Ed, ventured squintingly into the sun.

"That's right," Audrey said. "We grew up together in the Heights, and I'm awfully glad to see her again. I'm real glad to meet you boys, too. Your mother's told me an awful lot about you in her letters."

"Where do you live?" Ed asked.

"We've been living out West. We went out there for Walter's work. But now we're back."

"Oh."

"That's Dick, over there, of course," Moose's mother said.

Moose's father had gone to the other side of the drive to greet Walter.

"Here's my brood," Audrey said, gesturing toward the Plymouth.

The Mecklin kids, Frank and Lucy, had stepped sheepishly out the back of the car, one from each door; they now stood as if stricken in the blank afternoon light. Like their parents, they were tall and lanky; in fact, the entire family were giants, and they all shared the same squarish awkwardness. They resembled a troop of ungainly water birds, Moose thought, great storks or cranes, and he half expected them to wander down the dirt road and wade together into the swamp.

Wade they did not, however. Instead the adults went chatting into the house, leaving the children to their own devices. After some initial, awkward chit-chat, Moose and his brothers brought Frank and Lucy to the stout cherry tree on the edge of the yard. Having exhausted, after twenty or thirty minutes, all possibilities of climbing, clinging, scaling, and dangling, they took them around back to look for toads under the woodpile. Not having any luck at this, they worked the concrete lid off the well and peered deeply into its mute blackness for a while. Frank wanted to climb inside, make his way down the wrought iron ladder into the inviting darkness, but Moose and his brothers quickly squelched the idea. Their father had pronounced his most dire warnings against any such breach of the well shaft.

As Moose and his brothers stood looking hapless, Lucy, shifting on her feet, suggested a game of tag. Feeling sorry for her—she being the only girl in the group—the boys consented, and they spent half an hour chasing one another around the yard, the mongrel dog joining in at haphazard intervals. There was only one flare-up of Moose's famous temper; it was not, however, sufficiently exorbitant to elicit the customary chanting of his sometime sobriquet, "frenzy boy," by his brothers.

When Lucy said that she was warm, in the same drawly voice as her mother (only higher pitched), the kids all trooped inside to find lemonade or sodas. Entering through the basement door into the laundry room, they crossed the dark blue linoleum that to Moose always beckoned like some deep and mysterious sea, into the rec room. The adults were already there, where it was cooler in the days before Moose's father installed an air-conditioner upstairs. They were sipping drinks and chatting.

"Well, look what the cat drug in," Audrey said as the sweaty kids poured into the room.

Frank Mecklin slouched against the mantelpiece. Lucy looked blankly at her mother and drawled, "It's awful hot out there."

"I'll get some lemonade," Moose's mother piped up. "Ed, help me bring down some glasses."

Ed followed his mother upstairs while the other kids settled onto the low, sixties-modern furniture. Their arrival, and the departure of Moose's mother, occasioned a lull in which they sat catching their breath in the shallow panting of children.

It was at this caesura that Moose took close notice of Walter Mecklin for the first time. Moving a swizzle stick lazily in his drink, Walter gazed vaguely toward the floor. There was something different about the look of him—different, that is, than the blue-collar and country men Moose had grown up around. His chestnut hair undulated back in gentle ripples from his high, broad forehead. Behind his glasses (glasses!) was a pair of softly liquid eyes. His chin was just a thought, and there was a puckered quality about the set of his mouth. The shirt he wore draped gracefully over his frame, and its rich brown fabric sported a delicate pattern of wavy black lines. All in all, he presented a striking contrast to Moose's father, who possessed the raw country-boy masculinity of a young Steve McQueen.

Walter sensed Moose observing him, or perhaps he simply felt uncomfortable in the silence that followed the departure of Moose's mother. In any case, after stirring in his chair, and faintly clearing his throat, he addressed the boy.

"I understand you're studying the piano, young man."

Walter Mecklin's voice was as unusual, from Moose's point of view, as his appearance. There was a vaguely nasal quality to it, though the pitch was no higher than other men's, and he delivered his phrases at the same patient pace as his wife, with a sort of lisping lilt. If you didn't know better, you might have thought it an affectation.

"Yes sir," Moose replied, with the economy of expression characteristic of boys his age, brought up in the manner in which he had been brought up.

"He started lessons last year with one of the neighbors," Moose's father put in. "He seems to be doing pretty well."

"What are you playing?" Walter asked Moose. "Bach? Mozart?"

"Teaching Little Fingers to Play," Moose replied. He went to the piano to retrieve the red and white primer for Walter's perusal.

"Hmm," Walter intoned, quietly turning over the pages. "'In a Wigwam,' 'On the Trail,' 'Many Good Fish in the Sea' . . ."

"Oh Walter!" Moose's mother suddenly blurted, whisking down the stairs with a pitcher of lemonade. "That reminds me. I wonder if you could take a look at the piano, tell us what you think. We bought it second hand."

"I don't know if you want to get him started, Maug," Audrey said by way of warning. "Once he sits down at that keyboard . . ."

"Naw," Moose's father said, "we'd love to hear somebody put it through its paces."

"Since you ask," Walter began slowly. He rose from the sofa and moved toward the instrument. "Let's take a look."

The piano dominated the room from its position against the open stairway. It was an old upright grand with sliding doors across the front that, when opened, allowed you to see into its workings: all the coppery strings and tripping felt hammers. Somewhere along the course of its long history, for reasons no one will ever know, someone had spray-painted it the sickly green of a hospital gown. Its keys were the yellowed fingernails of a chain smoker, but everything with the exception of a couple of notes in the lowest and highest octaves worked.

Walter brushed the fingers of one of his massive hands along the keys and then gave the seat of the darkly worn stool a couple of slow turns.

"Go ahead and play something, Walt," Moose's mother begged cheerfully. "Let's hear some of that old razzamatazz."

"You're really asking for it, Maug," Audrey put in.

Moose's mother laughed good-naturedly as she moved over to Walter. "Come on, Walt, for old time's sake. I'll go up and get some spoons."

She rushed back up the steps while Walter positioned himself with difficulty on the rickety stool, rump-working it backward to accommodate his long legs. Once satisfied with this operation, he squared himself up to the instrument and placed his hands carefully across the keys. Then, like the sudden flight of startled birds, a cascade of rippling, trebly notes came spilling out of the big green box. These sounds filled the room with something Moose had never before experienced, some new species of intoxicant joy!

Walter added a rollicking bass line and was soon vamping an introduction; Moose's mother came skipping down the steps with the spoons and gave two each to Audrey and Moose's father. Taking up a position by the piano, she glanced at Walter and, recognizing the tune with a broad, toothy smile, began to sing:

> *I wanna hear it again, I wanna hear it again,*
> *That ol' pie-ana roll blues,*

Sitting at the upright, my sweetie and me,
Pushing on the pedals, making sweet harmony.
When it goes plinkety plink, when it goes dinkety dink,
We cuddle closer it seems,
And while we kiss, kiss, kiss away all of our cares,
The player pie-ana plays razzamatazz . . .

When the song ended there was a flurry of laughter, and Moose noted how all of the adults' faces were flushed. As they exchanged excited remarks, Ed led Frank Mecklin quietly off to see his coin collection. Tad sat on the hearth petting the dog, and Lucy Mecklin lounged at her mother's feet, sipping lemonade while she fanned her face with her free hand. As for Moose, he remained at the end of the sofa, transfixed by the magician at the piano. It didn't take much encouragement to convince Walter to play another tune, and then another. When memory failed, Moose's mother pulled some well-worn songbooks from the top of the piano.

"Remember these?" she asked, holding the books before Walter.

"What have we got here?" He adjusted his glasses and took up the volumes.

"These were Daddy's old books."

"Ah, yes," he replied, looking over the covers.

"Remember Mr. Rauther's band, Walt?" Audrey put in.

"Of course I do. Banjo man, as I recall."

"That's right," Moose's mother said with obvious pride. "He always said it was his banjo got us through the Depression, not his painting business."

"He turned you into quite the dancer too, as I recall," Walter said, "taking you around to all those Odd Fellows dances."

Audrey turned to Moose's father. "I suppose I don't need to

tell you," she said, "but your wife was quite the stepper back of a day."

"He doesn't give a hoot about that," Moose's mother said dismissively, barely looking up from one of the songbooks she was glancing through. "I couldn't get him out dancing if his life depended on it. He'd rather play poker with the boys."

There was an awkward silence, until Walter cleared his throat and said, "How about another tune?" He pressed open one of the books and placed it on the music rest. "A one, and a two, and . . ."

Walter played on, and everyone sang, and then he played again and yet again until the dinner hour was approaching and the Mecklins, at Audrey's insistence, took their leave.

It had been an extraordinary afternoon for Moose. He had never seen music played like that, not in person, not in the very room where he stood. To be sure, his musical experiences had been many: parading with his brothers around the little square record player covered in blue cloth, a yellow disk spinnning out a Sousa march; watching the bouncing ball in the cartoons; singing in the church choir; hearing his mother haltingly pick out melodies from her father's old songbooks; the radio, television, the movies; his own fledgling efforts at the keyboard. But now he had experienced something of a different order. He had witnessed a mere mortal—right before his very eyes!—summon the gods of harmony and rhythm, and he marked the transformation that was worked upon everyone present, not least upon himself.

Yet it was the reaction of his mother that most fascinated him. She often sang to herself when she worked in the kitchen, a phenomenon endlessly reassuring to the young Moose. She had a nice voice, and even sounded something like Doris Day, whom she would have resembled had it not been for a more angular cast to her features. She understood how to impart proper phrasing to a melodic line, and she was able to modulate her vibrato to professional effect—a consequence, no doubt, of early exposure to her father's musical activities.

When Walter played, Moose saw that musicality of his mother's burst into full flower. In place of the quiet kitchen singing came an expression of untrammeled vitality, a sudden syncing with some larger, some deeper current of energy. The company of her old friends from the Heights, and Walter Mecklin's playing—by turns exuberant, sweet, or melancholy—appeared the catalyst of this transformation. The swamp and the fields, her husband and sons, had had her in their thrall; here was a vehicle of liberation, a sweet chariot swinging low. Something sprung back to life in her; and for Moose, the simple world of the Manor and its environs would never again mark the confines of his universe.

&&&

Come September Moose started the fifth grade with a new teacher. Mrs. Pruitt, tall and blond, required her students to apply themselves, but her attitude was always friendly and collegial. Moose was fortunate in her. She recognized his affinity for artistic things, and she encouraged him in his drawings, his poems, and his stories. His most essential nature, which had theretofore regarded school chiefly as a set of rules to be followed upon pain of punishment (and as such, an extension of the regime established by his father at home) now experienced academe as a beckoning, nurturing force: one which offered a glimpse at how he might integrate a dream-bound personality into a society which had not yet presented any point of entry. His piano lessons with Mrs. Franklin went on apace—he

graduated from *Teaching Little Fingers to Play* to Book One of *John Thompson's Piano Course*—even if he had to fend off challenges from toughs at the bus stop who contended that piano lessons were for sissies. In one such instance he was thrown into one of his famous "frenzies" and had to be bodily restrained by his brothers, but not until he had furiously pummeled the aspiring greasers' ringleader.

The Mecklins continued their visits throughout the fall and winter, and inevitably Walter wound up at the piano. Moose never missed these sessions, though Ed would remain outdoors to throw rocks or climb into the cherry tree with Frank, while Tad and Lucy repaired to a corner of the rec room with cards or a board game.

Walter was a quiet showman, but he possessed some inexhaustible fire inside. His forte was the great heyday of Tin Pan Alley, when 28th Street in Manhattan rang with the sounds of America's popular music being forged. Have you ever heard, reader, things like "Bye, Bye, Blackbird," "Yes, Sir, That's My Baby," "Five Foot Two, Eyes of Blue," or "For Me and My Gal?" The fact that Walter seldom ventured into the more sophisticated music in which that era culminated—Cole Porter, the Gershwin brothers, or the even more urbane offerings of Jimmy Van Heusen and Sammy Cahn—reflected the proletarian roots of both him and his audience.

When he was in a loquacious mood, Walter would comment on the songs and their composers . . .

"I'm Looking Over a Four Leaf Clover," he announced one Saturday afternoon, thoughtfully perusing a songbook Moose's mother had opened before him. "—Composed by Harry Woods." He patted down the edges of the music book's pages as he went on. "Interesting man, Woods. Born with no fingers on his left hand." Walter turned up his own hand, gazed meditatively upon it for a moment. "Still managed to play quite a bass line, though, from what they say."

"That's real interesting, Walt," Audrey said, "but I don't know if it's what I'd call appropriate." She gestured, with a hike of her shoulders, towards the kids.

"Not appropriate?" Walter swiveled slowly on the stool, looked quizzically over his glasses. Turning toward Moose, he resumed *sotto voce*: "Harvard man, Woods was. Known to get into a scrap or two in a Bowery saloon. Now, that was only when he was in his cups . . ."

"Walter! Can we knock it off?"

"Knock it off?" He turned back to the keyboard and began to play before Audrey could comment further.

After the revelers had brought the corny standard's final, uplifting stanza to its rousing conclusion—"that I overlooked before!"—Walter leafed again through the pages of the song-book in quest of another selection. "How about 'Rock-a-Bye My Baby with a Dixie Melody?'" he asked.

"Oh boy!" Moose's mother chirped.

"Al Jolson hit," Walter remarked, easing back the stool to look over the score. He twisted toward his friends, spoke over one shoulder. "Did you all know that Jolson was a local Washington boy? No? That's right, he was. His father was a synagogue cantor, right here in town. Asa Yelson, that was Jolson's real name. I guess the talent promoters thought that sounded too, you know, 'Jewish' for public consumption . . ."

"Okay, Walter," Audrey said, with that trace of fatigue that often colored her voice, "can't we just play?"

"How about this one," Walter suggested when the jangling of the keys once again died out. "'Carolina in the Morning,' by Walter Donaldson. "Yes, nothing could be finer, than to be in Carolina, in the morning. The funny thing is, Donaldson never stepped foot out of New York City. I guess that just goes to show you . . ."

Over time Moose came to recognize the songbooks for what they were: sacred scriptures for a religion with no name. Of course the songbooks themselves had names: *Fabulous Hits of the Twenties, Fifty Fabulous Song Gems, Forty Hits of Our Time* (words and music with ukulele chords), *Forty-Four All-Time Hit Paraders.* They were, every one of them, chock full of music from the era of Moose's grandfather, music suffused with the flavor of ragtime piano and the tinny thrumming of banjo strings. It was a music rooted in the time before radio and the phonograph, when popular song was introduced on the vaudeville circuit and reproduced live at home; when there was a piano in every parlor—at least the parlor of every middle-class family. It was music that was, by design, meant to be played and sung, and so perfectly served the purposes of Moose's family and their friends the Mecklins. Most crucial for Moose, those old songs raised the spirit of a grandfather he had never known, forged a living connection to the man with the dapper stare and the banjo on his knee.

It didn't take long for Moose to grow familiar with the regular repertoire, and he soon knew many of the lyrics by heart. That repertoire was fixed in a more or less tacit manner, one that relied on a common intuition as to what was appropriate and what was not. Pages would be skipped over in silence, without anyone saying "Why don't we try that one," or "I remember that!" Some of the rejected tunes were merely outside the preferred style (straight ahead and forthright), like the subtly modulated expressions of Rodgers and Hart. Others were just plain offensive to the world-view of the participants—a worldview rooted in mainstream working-class culture, respectful of the premise that there is enough unavoidable unpleasantness in life for any right-minded person to add more of it to his existence in the guise of entertainment:

"Money is the Root of All Evil." Easily ruled out, along with any other reference to the dark side.

"Heartaches." Too unrelievedly sad.

"You're Just a Flower from an Old Bouquet." If you can't say anything nice about somebody, don't say anything at all.

"Comme Ci, Comme Ca." Couldn't pronounce it.

"Stars are the Window of Heaven." Came under the rubric "sappy."

"Rhumboogie." Suggests alcoholism.

"I'll Never Smile Again." Depressing.

"Sugar Blues." Sounds vaguely sexual. (Sex is private.)

"Mamma's Gone, Goodbye." This one required a glance over the lyric to effect a triage, a glance which quickly eliminated it: "I'm gonna get a man to treat me right/ One who'll stay home every night!"

"The Naughty Lady of Shady Lane." Requires no explanation.

"Secretly." They avoided secrets.

"Tom Dooley." Not interested in death.

"Vaya Con Dios." Nobody knew what it meant.

There were some titles Moose knew it was better not to ask about, like "Nobody Knows What a Red-Headed Mama Can Do."

In short, there soon developed, by common consent, an authorized liturgy, along with a vast but dark Apocrypha of which the existence was recognized, but that is all. The carolers' rejection of gritty themes was of a piece with the silence Moose's family observed in regard to his mother's late sister who, suffering from post-partum depression and an unfeeling husband, had blown her brains out with a shotgun; or the more distant murder of grandfather Gus's mother by his own father, who subsequently hanged himself in prison. By the same token, mention was never made of Gus's excessive drinking, his firey temper, or the occasional brawl at O'Brien's Bar on the Heights' main street. For, after all, how could people go on living, forging their paths through the world, if they were to constantly regurgitate the griefs that sliced at the heart like a razor, or the human failings that made life more difficult than it had to be? What's more to the point, how could one explain such things to a child, who only wanted to live, who wanted to know only happiness and safety?

Their philosophy, in music as in life, was "Always merry and bright!"

There was the occasional paradox, like the inclusion of the old chestnut, "Me and My Shadow," in a repertory that scrupulously avoided sadness. But this anomaly is explained by the masterful, and by no means hopeless, melody; and by the fact that, although the song addresses a man's loneliness, it posits a companion for him in the person of his own shadow. Sometimes, following his secret inner fires, Walter would stray outside the authorized scripture and play something moody, like "Body and Soul" or "Stardust." This would leave everyone feeling depleted and blue, or just plain confused. In such instances resort could be had to a rousing rendition of "Red Red Robin":

> *When the Red Red Robin,*
> *Comes bob bob bobbin' along,*
> *There'll be no more sobbin'*
> *when he starts throbbin' his old, sweet song,*
> *Wake up, wake up you sleepy head,*
> *Get up, get up, get outta bed,*

Cheer up, cheer up, the sun is red,
Live, love, laugh and be happy!'
&&&

Throughout the autumn and winter of Moose's tenth year, no momentous events occurred to mark the passage of time: no puppies were born, no small animals burned, no one died. Sally Hinneman was persuaded by the boys at the end of Rosemont Street to stand with her legs apart while they lay on the ground and gazed at her underpants, but if Moose learned anything from that breathtaking experience, he could not put a name to it.

His family's association with the Mecklins remained the chief novelty in Moose's existence, an association that affected every member of his household in one manner or another. Moose himself began to invest his playing with greater feeling and a budding sense of confidence. His temper was not so easily touched off; he was even able, on occasion, to parry taunts at the bus stop with sly insults rather than fists. His mother was less prone to outbursts, and when she stood at the stove mornings, the melodies that wafted down the rambler's narrow hallway with the smell of frying bacon had a new bounce to them. Moose's father occasionally asked his dependants to do something rather than ordering them, and he was even persuaded to take his wife dancing a couple of times. Ed's association with Frank Mecklin—who, older than Ed, ran wild outside the supervision of his father, who was invariably fixed at the piano—accentuated an already developing independence from Moose's parents. Youngest Tad, abandoned by Ed and Frank, with Moose lost in Walter's music, was left with no company but Lucy. He previsioned for the first time that, sooner or later, he would have to go it alone.

I Wanna Hear It Again

When the weather began to break with the coming of spring, another new visitor appeared in the neighborhood. This alien presence would make a profound impression on Moose, though it was only later that he came to see its advent as a totemic event, its disappearance as some kind of augury.

He had walked down the old farm road after school. His homework and piano practice were done and dusk was setting in. Peering across the swamp through the trees that lined the road, he glimpsed what seemed a fantastic vision: a great blue heron stepped daintily around the verges of the marsh, stalking its prey. Moose had never seen such a bird! Everything from its leaden blue coloring, to the aura of latent power it exuded, fascinated him. It seemed indelibly part of the landscape—and yet a bridge to some other world. In its aching combination of awkwardness and grace, Moose saw his own life revealed.

The bird remained around the neighborhood throughout early spring, and Moose hiked down the road almost daily to try and sight it. Sometimes the bird was not in evidence but would return the next day, or the day after. On a couple of occasions Moose spotted the heron out in the fallow fields that lay on the other side of the farm road from the swamp. And one incredible afternoon he startled it feeding at the road's margin, where there was a deep pool of open water. As it rose majestically before him, he could feel the sucking backdraft of its thwopping wings.

As the days grew longer with the swelling springtime Moose's sightings diminished, until finally he saw the bird no more. The ancient migratory patterns that had brought the wayfarer to the neighborhood now beckoned it onward to some further harbor. After many days without a sighting, Moose quit searching. Little League baseball was getting started, and the lengthening afternoons brought with them other commitments and other pleasures.

The Mecklins continued their Saturday visits, and Moose now began to watch Walter's hands more carefully, imagining how he too might make the big green box ring that way. He spent more time practicing, and even embarked on an exploration of his grandfather's old songbooks. His playing was newly informed with an eager energy he had never before experienced. Often, while working through a piece, an image of the big blue heron would flash across his mind, and that vision would spur him on.

Life was good for Moose that spring. Inspired by the genius of Walter Mecklin, charged with a flighted vision, he was coming out of the awkward malaise that had so afflicted him during his ninth year.

And then one Saturday, at the close of a visit marked by musical revelry of unparalleled gaity, the Mecklins announced that they were moving away. It was just that sudden. All Moose understood was that the reason had something to do with Walter's work.

They left in the heart of summer, which was fortunate for Moose, as that bright, carefree season offered myriad consolations to his wounded soul. Not only Audrey, but Moose's mother openly cried at their parting, which took place along the same phlox-lined drive where Moose first saw the Mecklin family the year before. Truth be told, Moose's eyes were not completely dry, nor those of his father or Tad. Only Ed, after casting a few last rocks into the woods with Frank, sported a manly cool as the big ugly Plymouth backed out of the gravel drive and slowly disappeared into the glaring asphalt of Rosemont Street.

Moose saw the Mecklins on other occasions during his childhood, when they visited from Chicago during summer vacations. They would reprise the old music, and Moose would sing along without a glance at the lyrics. As he grew into his teens, and his playing gained mastery, he would even take a turn at the keyboard himself, woodshedding through the tattered songbooks while the gang sang along behind him. Those jaunty, bouncing tunes of his grandfather's day had become indelibly printed on his soul; and in the days to come, long after he became a man, he would be buoyed through even his most trying moments by a subterranean current that would never run dry:

> *What if I've been blue,*
> *now I'm walking through fields of flowers,*
> *The rain may glisten, but still I'll listen,*
> *For hours and hours,*
> *I'm just a kid again, doing what I did again—*
> *Singin' a song,*
> *When the red, red robin comes bob, bob bobbin' along . . .*

Hawaii Blue

IT IS AN EXTRAORDINARY SOUND those palm trees make. Like a clicking, though Roger calls it a *ticking*. The ticking of the fronds, he says. I guess that is a good word for it. It's like a clock, sort of. It's such a delicate sound, who would notice it, unless you were someone like Roger, someone who sits out here at the crack of dawn *musing* or something. It's so quiet now, that's why I'm noticing it. Everyone's gone except me and HIM. He's upstairs, napping. Thank God he's gone to sleep. Thank God for another thing, too—this chaise lounge, right here by the water. All I want to do is rest.

It's hard for them to understand that.

What's all this about? It's about my family, all my families, and this new life inside of me. I've had plenty of time to think while everyone's out gallivanting around volcanoes and waterfalls (to the extent I can think at all, that is, with the lack of sleep and nausea). The jet lag doesn't help, though I never know what time it is anyway. Don't get me wrong, I'm not complaining about their going off. I'm glad they're having fun. I just want peace, quiet, and rest, and for HIM to sleep.

I'm happy about the leis, anyway. At least I had the presence of mind for that. Since Dan and I were the first ones here, it seemed like a duty or something. They were just the chintzy artifical ones, but it's the thought that counts, isn't it? Isn't it? I could tell that Dad liked it, and I know Roger's a sucker for that kind of ritual stuff. I felt more like a daughter and a sister again. That was good. This wife and mother business is kicking my butt.

Now that the Roger fiasco is over, everyone can relax again—to the extent that this group can relax, anyway. I was sitting right here in this chaise lounge when the whole episode started. It was first thing yesterday morning. Only Roger and I were up, I, because I never sleep anymore, and Roger, well, because he's Roger. When I first came down he was over there on the terrace doing yoga or something. Chilling the way he does. Then he must have gone in and gotten his swim trunks, because the next I know he was over the seawall. It's pretty shallow out there for quite a ways, and the water's so clear you can see all the coral formations on the bottom. The usual bunch of boats were out there, that big navy ship, and all the other ones of different shapes and sizes. I watched Roger step over the coral with his arms out to his sides, balancing himself like he was flying or something.

"How's the water?" I called out.

"Great," he hollered back. "Perfect day for bananafish!"

"What the heck is that?"

"Never mind," he yelled and just kept walking.

I watched him get smaller and smaller, he must have gone out a mile. I figured he was trying to get to where it was deep enough to swim. It looked like he was going to walk clear over to Lanai—or Molokai. We never did get straight which island that closer one is. Then HE started to fuss, and I went back upstairs to check on him.

I wonder what SHE is thinking. Or if she thinks anything yet. I'm assuming it's a she. That would make Dad happy, his first biological granddaughter. I wouldn't mind, either. I can only imagine what she'll think of this bunch. I wonder if she's enjoying herself, if she knows she's in Hawaii, if she can feel this blue, this clear light. I hope she sleeps better than HIM. They all make fun of me for driving him around in the minivan to make him sleep, but they don't have to put up with him all night like I do.

The plane ride just about killed me. All night in the air and HE didn't sleep a wink. I don't see why they have to be so picky about the rules. After I managed to get seats at the bulkhead, so he'd be able to lie on the floor, then they wouldn't let him. It's beautiful here and all, but like I told Dan, it's an awful long haul to the beach when Ocean City is just three hours from home. I know it's a big deal for Dad, and I can't believe the bucks he spent on this place. Fourteen thousand smackers per week for two weeks. I'm sure he could find more prudent things to do with his retirement money.

Sometimes the old man is just like a big kid. But in some weird way, I've got to admit, it's that kid-ness of his that keeps us all going. Those monthly horseback riding adventures he organized, after Mom kicked him out, may have been part of a determined campaign to stay involved in the lives of his children, but it was he who most relished galloping across Southern Maryland fields and meadows, bringing some bucking steed to heel. And when the bros break out their guitars and hand drums for a family sing-along, who always sings the loudest? Who never fails to request "Rocky Raccoon?"

His lust for life is infectious.

Too bad they couldn't get someone out here to clean the carpet before he arrived. That damn volcano dust is everywhere. This whole island is crumbling, that's what it comes down to. Falling apart. The entire place is made of pumice. Turning to dust and blowing away, before your very eyes!

The snorkeling was a good thing, at least. I did make it to

that adventure. Roger called it a "small moment of grace," whatever that meant. I don't go in for any religious mumbo jumbo. Maybe he meant that it was a good bonding experience. It's true we were on the verge of a family dysfunction meltdown.

But really, should anyone have been surprised that oldest Charles immediately tried to organize everybody, and that youngest Bo resented it; that acutely sensitive middle Roger got on Dad's nerves with his subtleties, and then got annoyed with the old fart for not understanding him; or that Dan quickly grew sick of my family's bossiness, as he calls it (or Dad always making jokes—Dad thinks they're funny—at his expense)? He's so touchy. What about me? I'm basically so tired and just plain sick, I don't really give a crap about anything. Except please don't wake HIM after I've finally put him to sleep. It would also be nice if they would come and fix the fricking pool cover so I don't have to worry about my son drowning all the time. Of course Terri makes a big racket at the pool while HE's napping, and then she gets indignant and sulks when I shush her (maybe that was a little rude) and no one can get anybody out here to fix the damn pool cover.

What is it with that agent?

Like I said, the snorkeling did seem to help. The way we swam around the cove like a school of fish seemed to make us feel more cohesive. Also the wonder of the beauty. If we could be as dumb—or smart—as fish, it would be better. Just swim around and eat all the time.

Hope the sharks don't find you.

Roger got into the whole aloha thing, which is so like him. Peace and love and sharing and togetherness. All that hippy stuff he's always been into in one form or another, whether it's yoga, meditation, poetry, spiritual, whatever. I know him. I know his ways. We're actually a lot alike. Only I'm more practical, which, being a woman, I don't have much choice, do I? Let's face it, if it were up to men to take care of the serious business of this world, we'd all be up poop's creek and no paddle.

Right?

Roger's a dreamer. He takes things to heart and then he won't let them go.

"This family's a real case, isn't it?" he said while we were sitting near the sea wall the evening before he disappeared.

"You're telling me."

"Everybody plays their roles like they're on auto-pilot, without the least clue about how it affects anybody else. I guess that includes me."

"I don't think you're bothering anybody in particular."

"We had a full-on mutiny on our hands the other day."

"You mean with Bo and Charles?"

"Yeah. Bo was so upset about Charles planning everything without consulting anybody, he and Terri threatened to take one of the minivans on a counter-excursion. It's all just to prove a point, if you ask me. Bo still hasn't gotten over how Charles and I used to tie him to the tetherball pole when we were kids."

I laughed. "It wouldn't have been so bad if you hadn't played tetherball while he was there."

"I can understand his resentment," Roger said, his low, throaty laugh bleeding through. "But isn't it high time he get over it? Let it go?"

"Charles seems to be easing off on the agendas," I said.

"I talked to him yesterday about having meetings after dinner to sort out the next day's plans, so everyone could have some input. Personally, I don't much care where we go. I realize everyone doesn't have to go everywhere together. But what's the point of everybody converging on one place, which is a pretty rare event, if we treat it like so many separate vacations?

Dad invested a lot of anticipation in this thing, after all, not to mention a sizable chunk of his retirement pay-out. I think he'd be pleased if we stick together for at least the occasional main event."

"I just had a weird thought," I said suddenly, responding to I-don't-know-what soundings of memory. "I wonder how it would be if Mom were here. You know, if she and Dad were still together."

Our parents—and the rest of us with them—went through a bitter, wrenching divorce when we were teenagers. Roger, the oldest of my brothers still at home, bore the brunt of it. My mother's late-night, chain-smoking-fueled ramblings. My father's desperate suicide attempt . . .

"One big, happy family, huh?"

"I'm not saying it would be perfect. But even after so many years, it just seems odd we're all here together, and she's not with us."

"I guess I know what you mean. And maybe that explains all the dysfunction. We still haven't accepted the broken symmetry at the heart of our family. We keep acting the way we've always acted, reprising old roles, in the hope that the ancient togetherness will magically return. It's like some kind of cargo cult. We have no earth mother at our core, that steady, nurturing force . . ."

"I have no idea what a cargo cult is," I said. "But as for the earth mother bit, sometimes I feel like I've taken on that role for everybody. And I've got to tell you, brother, it's getting to be too much for me. Especially now."

I patted my distended belly.

"You've got plenty on your hands. In other places, too . . ."

We sat staring into the ocean for a while.

"Have you talked to Bethann?" I asked him.

Bethann is Roger's wife. They've been separated for upwards of a year.

"A couple of weeks ago."

"She still sleeping with that bozo?"

"Yep. I've about given up on that one."

"I think it's time, brother."

"I agree."

"Are you taking it okay?"

"I'm fine," he said. "The worst part is the way it drags up Mom and Dad's horrible divorce. I feel like I'm repeating the same, sad pattern . . ."

He choked up a little, but then spoke as calmly as can be. "Charles' kids seem to be having a good time."

"Why wouldn't they? They get to hang out in a Lahaina villa for free. Cruise the strip and go surfing. A couple of them are definitely on dope."

"The snorkeling was a small moment of grace, at least," he mused, looking off into the blue. "Everybody seemed to gel a little better."

"Where is it that you all went today? Mount hocky-locky-looky or something? How was that?"

"It's too bad you weren't there," he said, suddenly all jazzed up the way he gets. "We started up Mount Haleakala, early this morning, under a complete cloud cover. But at about, oh, seven thousand feet, we broke through to this clear, bright light. From that point forward, as we wound along the mountain road, there was an unbroken floor of cloud below us. It was just like when you're flying in an airplane. There's this huge crater at the top, at ten thousand feet. It resembles a lunar landscape up there. The light is so pure, it was like being in another world. And when you looked offshore, the brilliant blue of the ocean sparkled through the breaks in the cloud cover. Something incredible happened to me, just being up there. There was a sense of opening up to the world. Of drawing all of its power, majesty, and beauty into my very being."

"It sounds lovely. But I'm sure I could have never made it, the way I'm feeling."

We sat in silence again, listening to the palms ticking.

"What are you doing tomorrow?" I asked.

"I don't know," he said. "Maybe I'll walk over to this café on the strip. A local band is playing there. I heard a bit of their act yesterday, and I was highly impressed. They do this traditional Hawaiian stuff and, to be honest, it was a bit of a revelation for me."

"Are you talking about that jungle-sounding hoopla, with all the drums? And the unintelligible chanting? I think that stuff is kinda weird, if you want to know my opinion."

"I can see how the ceremonials would strike the average mainlander as odd. But this group also does some modern Hawaiian tunes. Of the more tasteful sort, of course. They've got some great slack-key guitar work."

"I wouldn't know a slack key from a frack key," I said.

"Sis," he began in his big brother voice, "there's a whole world of modern Hawaiian music out there, even if us *haoles* aren't aware of it. These guys at the café played one tune, in particular, that really floored me."

"Yeah?" I didn't bother to ask what *haole* meant.

"I've just about worked it out on the ol' git."

"Could you play it for me?" I asked. I knew he wanted to and besides, I was tired of talking. A little passive entertainment sounded like a great way to end the evening.

He went over to his side of the compound and came back with his instrument.

"It's a little rough," he said as he sat down again.

"I'll use my imagination."

He spread a piece of paper on the chaise beside him. "I found the lyric online and copied it out," he said. "Apparently this tune has become something of a classic here in the islands." He started to finger-pick some chords and then said, "I think it really sums up the whole Hawaiian *zeitgeist*" (whatever that is). He stared intently at his fingers as he riffed nimbly over the strings. "You know," he went on, "the togetherness. An abiding commitment to one's relations. Rootedness in earth and home . . ."

He picked the chords a little longer and then, looking out over the water began, in his scratchy baritone, to softly sing. The song was deeply nostalgic. Its protagonist, who has left the Hawaiian Islands, addresses a sister who has stayed behind. The brother recalls the happy times of his youth, when they rode horses in the hills, caught some fish called wapu (or something) in mountain streams, and sang together through the balmy tropical evenings. Just the previous night, he confides, he had dreamt that he was returning home. But he finds himself beset by fears that his sister will no longer be the same companion he once shared so much of life with, nor he the brother she once had known. "You have lingered there," Roger sang, "but I no longer can, it seems."[1]

There was more to it, but that's all I can report, because somewhere around the middle of the song I went dead out. Listening to my brother sing and play, one of the happier memories of my youth, was so calming that the chronic exhaustion finally caught up to me. I'm sure all that crooning about dreaming didn't help, either. When I came to, who knows how much later, Roger was sitting there, softly picking out some other tune.

"It looks like my song was a real knock-out," he quipped

---

[1] The lines are from "Me ke aloha ku'u home o Kahalu'u," by Jerry Santos. Translation: "with love of my home of Kahalu'u."

with his gentle laugh.

"It was sweet. And very relaxing."

"I'm glad to be of service."

"I guess I'll go up to bed."

"I think I'll just sit out here awhile," he said.

"Listening to those palms ticking?"

"Whatev."

"Don't go getting all nostalgic on me."

"Don't worry, Sis. Have a good night."

He sounded fine. But as I climbed the steps to my family's suite, I couldn't help worry about him. Sitting alone in the night while his siblings all nestled in with their honeys. I could only hope that he wouldn't fall into some kind of melancholy jag. Like I said, he gets too caught up in life's sadnesses, takes things to heart. He's been admirably stable since his nervous breakdown, back before he and Bethann got married. But since she ran off with that yoga instructor, we've all grown concerned about him again. What, because the guy gave her some Hindu statue or something? With eight arms? I don't get it. That's what happens, I always say, when you get involved in a bunch of mumbo-jumbo. I'm sure Roger knows we worry over him (he's no dummy) but he goes right on with his usual stuff. Cafés and songs, poetry, yoga . . .

All that Roger sort of stuff.

Be all that as it may, I wasn't able to devote much time to fretting about my brother, since when I arrived at my family's suite I had to calm Dan down, because of course Dad hurt his feelings at Mount Hocky-Docky with some crack that was supposed to be humorous. That only made him more frustrated that he couldn't work in his deep-sea fishing trip, the one thing he really wanted to do while we were in Hawaii.

Well, the next morning everyone was out on the terrace

having a late breakfast (except me, of course, because the mere thought of food turns my stomach) and someone remarked that Roger wasn't around. I said that I had seen him wade out into the ocean at first light.

"And you know what," I added, "he said something really weird."

"What was that?" Charles asked.

"When I asked how the water was, he said it was a 'perfect day for bananafish,' whatever that is. What is a bananafish, anyway? Some kind of tropical species?"

"The only bananafish I know of," Charles started explaining in his first-born-son way, "is from a story by J.D. Salinger. In fact, 'A Perfect Day for Bananafish' is the story's title."

"Really?"

"Yeah," Charles said as he settled back in his chair. I could see that his mind was roving through its awesome filing system, pulling up some fact the way he goes through the tax code seeking information for his law clients. "As I recall," he began, "the story centers around this guy who's supposed to be J.D. Salinger's older brother, Seymour. Let's see. He's staying at some resort in Florida. And he somehow develops a touching—and cutely whimsical—relationship with this little girl he meets on the beach. The background—this has already been developed by Salinger—is that Seymour is trapped in a marriage that lacks both understanding and any real affection. At one point they have this huge row in the hotel suite. . ."

"But where does the bananafish come in?"

Charles began to braid the fingers of his hands in and out of one another, concentrating like that. "If I recall correctly," he said, "the Seymour character is out in the ocean swimming with this little girl—the one he met on the beach. He teases her about the bananafish, saying it's such a perfect day for them and all. Of course, he's completely making the whole thing up. I don't think there's even such a thing as a bananafish."

Charles looked vaguely toward the water, that placid smile of his spread across his face.

"Wait," I said, "that's it? That's the whole story?"

"No," Charles said soberly. "Actually, the story has a pretty unpleasant ending. Are you sure you want to hear it?"

"Unpleasant is the story of my life these days." I patted my belly.

He looked out toward the water again, but now his smile had morphed into a sort of pained grimace. "After going swimming with this cute little girl," he said, visibly flinching as he said it, "the Seymour character goes up to his room and blows his brains out with a .38 caliber revolver."

"Jeez, that's gross! Why would anyone write a story like that?"

"I don't know," Charles said. "It could be that Salinger's own brother committed suicide, and that was his way of dealing with it. I've never really looked into it."

One of Charles's kids suddenly blurted something about going surfing, and everybody got onto how they were going to spend the day.

Me, I started to worry about Roger again. Why, I asked myself, would he say that about the bananafish? The nausea and hormones and lack of sleep were no doubt playing on me, but I began to grow increasingly paranoid. I recalled our conversation of the previous evening, with the family dysfunction, Beth-ann running off with some swami wannabe, the echos of our own broken family. Then there was that song he sang. Beautiful, but achingly poignant. What was that line?

And you have lingered there my sister,
But I no longer can, it seems.

What if he's gotten into some kind of melancholy jag, I thought to myself. Another depression? What if he up and decided to do something desperate?

As everybody wandered off, still discussing various tropical adventures, I sidled up to Charles. "You don't think Roger would do anything . . . crazy, do you?"

"Crazy? What do you mean?"

"You know, desperate."

"Like what?"

"Like"—I brought my voice to a whisper—"suicide."

"Suicide? Why would you say that?"

"It seems to run in the family, for one thing," I whispered. "Then there's this whole thing with Bethann. Last night he told me he had flat out given up on their marriage."

"About time," Charles said. "He seems pretty normal to me. I don't think he'd do anything like that."

"I know one thing," I said. "I saw him wade out toward those islands this morning, and I never saw him come back. And what about those bananafish? Saying crazy things from a story about some guy who kills himself because his wife doesn't understand him!"

"Are you sure no one else has seen him?"

"I don't know. I'll go and check."

I went in the main house and asked around. The teenagers were splayed across the sofas like they do every morning. Morning for them, of course, meaning high noon. It seemed no one had seen Roger. Just me, wading out over the corals. Peeking into his room, I didn't see his wet trunks anywhere. Growing more nervous by the minute, I went back out on the terrace.

"I'm still concerned about Roger," I said to Charles. "I don't see his trunks anywhere."

"I wouldn't trouble yourself about it," Charles said in his

best legal advisor voice. "Roger knows how to take care of him-self."

Then it was time to feed HIM, so I went over to the smaller house on the other side of the pool, the one where my little family group was staying. It was quiet now and after he nursed, I thought, maybe he would fall asleep. Then I could take a nap.

But watching HIS puckered mouth eagerly suck the life out of me got me feeling more mothery by the minute, and my worries about my silly brother went into overdrive. Who knows what a person might do, I thought, if he gets too caught up in the inevitable sadnesses of life? Sure, Charles said not to worry. But Charles, with that number-one-son, can-do optimism of his, has never really understood the pits of emotional darkness the rest of us can sometimes fall into.

After I put HIM down, I went over to the main house again and no one was there. I had talked Dan into scheduling his fishing trip, so he would finally quit complaining, and he had been gone since before dawn. It was anybody's guess where the others had gotten off to.

I came out here to this chaise lounge and sat looking over the water. It was real quiet. I could hear those fronds ticking, just the way Roger said, and before long it was an established fact that he was out there somewhere. Out in all that blue. Lost. Finally, unable to stand it anymore, I went in and called 911. My voice was all quivery, and I suppose they took me serious-ly, because pretty soon there were Coast Guard boats cruising around. Even, hovering overhead, a helicopter.

After an hour or so Dad came along with some of the others. When I told them my theory about Roger, and that I had called 911, they put on a collective expression of skepticism. They didn't say it, but I could tell they thought I was overreacting. I don't know how that made me feel. A little sheepish, I suppose.

They all joined me on the terrace just the same, watching the boats and the helicopter, discussing them at first like it didn't have anything to do with anyone we knew. But after a while, with all that serious action going on out there, I could see that they were also starting to become a little anxious. They grew very quiet, ominous sort of, and every now and then Charles or Bo would get up and pace back and forth like a caged jaguar.

The teenagers went into town to search the cafés on the strip, but they returned an hour later with nothing good to report. In the middle of the afternoon a couple of police officers came out and spoke to Dad and Charles and me. They had also searched the various hang-out spots and come up empty-handed. It was all I could do to hold back my tears.

And then, after all that—wouldn't you know it?—my silly brother Roger (it was about five in the afternoon) comes sauntering onto the terrace, looking happy as some Hawaiian clam.

"What's all that hubbub out there?" He gestured toward the water. The boats, the helicopter . . .

Bo and Charles rushed over to him. "We were worried as all hell about you, Bro," Bo said.

"Worried? What do you mean?"

They explained what was going on. I stood by, listening.

"I'm sorry," Roger said. "I didn't mean to worry anyone."

"Why didn't you tell somebody where you were?" my father said gruffly. "Where on earth have you been?"

"I was just hanging with some new friends," Roger said. "I didn't know anybody would be looking for me."

I went over and gave him a big, stupid hug. So did Dad. "Don't be worrying us like that," he ordered in his father voice.

Roger's face tightened up, like he was about to tell the old man where he could get off. But he didn't. He just laughed and said that it was "nice to be missed."

I felt kind of stupid. But I don't care. Once you become a mother, you lose all sense of dignity anyway. Besides, what if he *had* been out there, and I didn't do anything? We all went out to dinner on the strip. To celebrate, sort of. When we returned, my brothers broke out their guitars. We had a wonderful evening, with the sea breeze and fun singing and fruity drinks.

It wasn't until first thing this morning that I was able to get the full scoop from Roger, out here at my chaise lounge. He had gone over to that café, just like he said he would. But when he got there he learned that the band he liked wasn't playing. He decided to take a stroll on the strip to see what else might be on offer, and as fate would have it, he ran into one of his favorite band guys on the street. Roger told him how much he enjoyed the band's music, they got into a conversation about frack key and other stuff Roger likes to talk about, and the guy invited him to head into the hills and hang out with him and his other musical friends.

"Can you believe it?" Roger said. "We went fishing in the mountains, just like in that song I played for you. One of the traditional spirit men was even there. A real kahuna! We did some incredible drumming and chanting. It was really something."

"I was so worried about you."

"Sis," he said, "I think you're losing it. Hormones, most likely. Look, I'm fine." He stretched his arms out to his sides, displaying his fine self. "Besides, no matter how bad things ever got, I'd never do *that* to you. Or to Mom or Dad. Or to Charles and Bo. Or the kids. Even that little one inside of you. God knows, there's enough horror in this world as it is."

We sat looking over the quiet morning ocean. For once in my life, I didn't know what to say.

"Life is so beautiful," Roger took up again. "Just look at all that blue out there. And if you listen real close, you can hear those fronds ticking. Ever so delicately . . ."

I felt something quicken inside of me. I don't know if it was HER shifting, or just plain nausea. The fronds were ticking away, like some kind of clock keeping some kind of other-time. What's that old song say? Does anybody really know what time it is?

All I can say is, aloha, and amen.

My Immortal Brother

I look back, ransack memory for an augury, some sign or wonder that might have portended it. We were seated around an oaken table at a country inn, enjoying an Easter luncheon, when my brother Ed disclosed the news: he would be *immortal*. Not that he put it exactly like that. He was telling us about Dr. Charles Barkwood's latest book, *No Time for Death*. "There's no reason anyone will have to die," he enthused. "According to the author—and he's no slouch—all you have to do is get through the next thirty years in relatively good health, and have the means to pay for the treatments. I mean, they're already growing human liver cells on hogs' livers. A lot of this stuff could be done today. With the development of nanobots, and further advances in bioengineering, there will be no disease that can't be cured. Even down to a simple age spot!"

Ed sat directly across the big round table from me. My sister Pooky was to one side of him with her little girl, Leigh. My mother sat next to them. On Ed's other side were his wife Deirdre (who was also scheming to cheat the grave), Pooky's husband, Dan, and he and Pooky's six-year-old, Gregory.

Gregory, clever kid that he is, had brought his portable chess set to the restaurant. He had hoped to engage me in a game, thereby avoid siting mutely by while adults discussed a lot of incomprehensible hooey. And now, in that simple way of his I'm really beginning to appreciate, his upward glance speaking a wordless invitation, he unceremoniously placed the board on the corner of the table. I had only begun to teach him a few weeks earlier, and he was still in the habit of trying to take pieces checkers-style, by hopping over them. But he was eager, in that unspoken way of his, to advance his knowledge of the game. Had he known that the man he refers to as Uncle Peen (a custom dating to my brother's habit, when Gregory was an infant, of calling him Peanut) was in the process of revealing his immortality (a modern-day Alexander the Great in the bosom of his own family!) he might have forgotten games for the moment and perked up to the conversation. As it was, he appeared unfazed by his uncle's impending apotheosis, preferring to investigate the subtleties of the knight's quirky leaps, the glorious power of the queen, or the humble but useful services of the pawns.

When Ed let out with the one about the age spot, Pooky shot me a glance, half worried, half bemused. I knew what she was thinking. Ed has always been a high achiever. He graduated at the top of his law school class and now, at midlife, was sitting on a considerable pile of lucre. I figured Pooky thought that while immortality might be a worthwhile goal, concern over a few age spots was overdoing it. She was banking on a long understanding between us regarding Ed: that his tendencies toward order, perfection, and self-discipline could be taken to extremes. It was also understood that he thought both of us woefully disorderly and excessively emotional. Perhaps, if not lazy, than at least improvident as well. At our Christmas gathering, while we all discussed our prospects for eventual retirement, he had said of me: "As little as Moose works, he'll never be able to retire!" Though I know he regretted the remark (he said nothing, but I know him well, the way he recoiled back upon himself), —and though there was probably more than a little plain, unvarnished truth in his words, it nonetheless stung.

Why can't we let each other be!

My mother, who was between Pooky and me, wearing a straw bonnet with an artificial flower attached, decided it was time to bring in the wisdom of the ages. "You know," she said, "when Great Grandma was in the nursing home, she used to tell me how all of her friends were gone. They'd all died, of course, because she had lived so long. Kate, she'd say, I don't have any reason to live. I'm just a holdover."

No spring chicken herself, my mother fell silent with a sudden sense of pathos.

Ed, for his part, brushed blithely past this possible crimp in his plans for eternal existence. "If we outlive everybody we know," he said in his inimitably practical, ever-optimistic way, "we'll just make new friends."

Ed is two years older than me, and my mother used to tell me how excited he was when I was born. He insisted on pushing my stroller, she would recount, and when we encountered passersby he would claim me as his own. "My baby, my baby!" he would say. "My baby!" Later, when he started elementary school, he liked to sit my brother Tad and me before a green chalkboard in our upstairs rumpus room and go over his lessons with us, imparting a precocious glimmer of our futures in academe. Our natural leader through countless war games and escapades, it was he who forged new paths through the woods and fields that surrounded our neighborhood, to the fishing pond or to the gravel pit; it was he who organized sandlot ball games and quarterbacked our football team. It was he also who bore the brunt of our father's discipline, a traditional, if unlonged-for, perk of many an eldest son.

Now he was telling us about his and Deirdre's private

consultations with Dr. Barkwood, author of *No Time for Death*.

"What?" Pooky erupted. "You go to the West Coast every other month just for a check-up?"

"It's quite a bit more than a typical check-up," Deirdre, who had worked as a nurse, explained. "They do extensive blood work, and a whole array of different scans."

"If you want a shot at these life-extending technologies," Ed came in, "which Barkwood expects to come on line in thirty years or so, you've got to keep your body in decent shape. If your organ systems are completely ravaged or, for that matter, you're aleady dead, you'll miss the boat."

"Yeah," Pooky rejoined, "but those constant trips out West, all those tests. Geez, it must cost a fortune!"

"It's not cheap," Ed conceded, "but it's worth it. After evaluating you, they carefully calibrate a whole slew of supplements to maintain the proper balances in your body. We take twenty different pills with every meal. In fact, that reminds me. Baby, did you remember to bring them?"

While Deirdre dug into her purse, the waiter showed up with the main course. Everybody oohed and aahed over the collection of supplements, of different shapes and colors, piled beside Ed and Deirdre's plates. As they swallowed these, Deirdre one at a time, elegantly, Ed in nonchalant handfuls, my hungry family plowed into their meals.

With everyone occupied for the moment, I tried to wrap my mind around Ed's astonishing announcement. Ranging back over the years we had lived as brothers, I remembered some lines I once composed (though I am no poet) about the riding stable where we worked together as teens: Pleasant Pastures Riding Academy. Ever industrious, Ed had answered an ad for stable hands, wishing to expand his income beyond the paper route he had run since the fourth grade. After a couple of years

My Immortal Brother

he brought me in, and we spent our weekends in the presence of those noble beasts—and even nobler companions:

> *Cut fields smelled of hay; they*
> *set me thinking of the old stable,*
> *where we mucked stalls and*
> *piled high with fodder, Commander Dirson's*
> *flatbed truck, with the brothers Blair:*
> *two Homeric heros who'd lost their way,*
> *in the wings of history, and wandered*
> *onto the strange stage of this century;*
> *my brother Ed was our Agamemnon . . .*

Yes, heroic he was, even godlike in those days! His hawk-like eyes and aquiline nose, erect bearing, his affability and confidence; his endless energy. When I picture him striding through the hallways of our high school, surrounded by friends, invariably in the middle of something purposeful, I see him in an aura of light. He was always a top student, a favorite of teachers also for his good manners and cooperative disposition. He was equally popular with his classmates, and was regularly elected class president.

Ed was the undisputed champion of those, like myself, who considered ourselves *collegiates*. We lived in uneasy coexistence with the *greasers*, rough kids who lived for their tricked-out cars, smoked cigarettes, slicked back their hair, hung chains from their belts, made their girlfriends pregnant and loved to fight— in gangs and with knives, or so our legends had it. Most of them were chronically held back in school, and they greatly resented those of us who appeared to be succeeding in the system.

The king of the greasers was a man (and I use the word advisedly, for he had reached the age of majority by his sophomore year) with the unlikely but appropriately scary name of Boo O'Hara. One Friday evening, while we were all at the weekly dance in the school's cafeteria, word came that Boo and his gang were planning to take Ed down a few notches. I was alarmed for my brother's safety, but Ed, positively delighted with this novel challenge, calmly proceeded to organize his own gang from among the school's wrestling squad (of which he was, of course, captain). I watched them surround him when he left the dance, sons of doctors and sons of mechanics, feisty bantams and heavyweight bruisers. They all loved Ed, considered it an honor to be part of his retinue. In the event, Boo and his greasers kept their distance, satisfying themselves with a little trash talk. What's more, the show of force seemed to have intimidated them permanently, for the threats against Ed ceased for good.

Remembering this episode, I was not surprised when, years later, Ed cooly disarmed a thug who held him at gunpoint in a deserted car park.

Ed was now just as cooly describing his and Deirdre's projected route to eternal life. "You really have to watch your glycerides," he said. "Just one muffin, for example, puts a huge glycemic load on your pancreas. And the free radicals, they're constantly tearing your body down. That's why Deirdre and I drink eight glasses of alkalized water every day."

The idea of all that alkalized water made my mother, who had worked as a medical secretary, decidedly nervous. "You'd better watch that," she said flatly.

"Eight glasses is nothing," Ed reassured her. "You'd need to drink eight gallons to have a systemic effect. The amount Deirdre and I ingest just alters the pH balance in the intestinal track. It scavenges the free radicals before they can get to the rest of your body."

"Alkalized?' Pooky, who was wiping Leigh's face, asked. "Is

that like Alka-Seltzer?"

"Plop plop, fizz fizz," I couldn't help quip, as Gregory tried to take my queen by moving a bishop sideways, "what a relief not having to die is!"

"Sorry, Ed," I said as the laughter subsided, in which he and Deirdre both unaffectedly joined. Ed didn't mind my interjecting a little levity, a staple at family gatherings, and my joke barely broke his stride. He went on to answer Pooky, while I quietly explained to Gregory the nature of the bishop, a character of great power who, like the rest of us, must nonetheless accept his limitations.

Ed was a great brother. That he enjoyed unapologetically some of the prerogatives of the eldest was to be expected; his many kindnesses were all his own. I remember my first date. The object of my attentions, who boarded her glossy bay hunter at the stable, was to be my companion at the ninth grade prom. It was Ed who saved me the signal embarrassment of having one of my parents drive us to the dance; instead he and Deirdre chauffeured us in the most gracious style imaginable. Though Ed and Deirdre were only a couple of years older than me, they existed on some mysterious plane far removed from my existence. There was a natural bounty about them that spilled onto all they encountered, a grandeur grounded in an awareness of others—and their own roles in their social milieu—that escaped my adolescent narcissism. Discreet yet friendly, Deirdre knew exactly how to talk to Wanda to make her feel comfortable; and I have always remembered that drive to the prom as a magical, fairy-tale journey. Charioted through a twilight dimension by otherworldly hosts, I felt a novel wonder when I placed my arm around Wanda's slender shoulders, knew the impossible softness of her cashmere sweater beneath my hand. Later, when

Ed went off to college, he bequeathed to me his motorcycle, roaring steed which now carried me to Wanda's house on dark winter evenings.

These and many other acts of generosity, toward me and others, will always color my picture of Ed. And I still feel close to him, despite the divergent paths we've taken as adults. When I dropped out of law school, determined to focus on my literary strivings, Ed did not hesitate to let me know that he considered my decision an improvident one—though I am certain he was already aware of the signal difference in our temperaments. In fact, it was during our youthful grand tour of the country, only a couple of years earlier, while viewing an exhibit of Van Gogh's paintings in Chicago, that he first found a name for everything about my character he had previously found incomprehensible: the "tortured artist syndrome." The great Dutchman's pained path through life, briefly recounted in the exhibit's placards, offered my brother a ready explanation for what had become of the baby he once claimed as his own, a baby who turned into a brooding adolescent, addicted to his books, piano, and records; an arrested adolescent who showed few signs of becoming a normal American adult.

My ears pricked up when I heard the word *opera*, among my many enthusiasms of that era. I left Gregory to consider his next move, while I turned my attention to the conversation going on around the table.

"I've never even seen an opera," Ed was saying. "Here I am at forty-six. According to actuarial tables, I'll live to eighty-four. That's thirty-eight more years. In other words, I've already lived more years than I have left to live. And what have I done? Exactly nothing."

"You've done plenty, if you ask me," Pooky rejoined spunkily. "You've raised a family. Your kids are marvelous. You've been a good husband and father and brother and son. You're extremely well-respected in your profession. Isn't your book on pension law a standard in the field?"

"I've seen *Aida* three times, at Toby's dinner theatre," my mother piped in. "And I was in *Carmen*. We did that one in the eleventh grade. I danced in the chorus!"

Ed took the occasion of my mother's remark to forestall things taking too serious a turn. "Look," he said lightly, "even Mom's ahead of me!"

But Ed's quip could not dispel the sense of pathos that struck me as I considered whether to take Gregory's queen, which he had gleefully—and prematurely—swept down the board to threaten my king. My brother Ed, anyone's paragon of success, had just announced that he considered his entire life a cipher. Were I feeling competitive, I might have felt vindicated in my own, divergent choices. While Ed kept his nose to the grindstone, being successful in the eyes of the world, I had allowed myself room for the arts, spiritual pursuits, close friendships, and extended journeys to exotic places—many of the things Ed now felt to be missing in his experiences. More importantly, I had allowed nothing to get in the way of my dream to shape words into works of power and beauty.

But I knew it wasn't that simple.

After dropping out of law school, I endured years of bitter struggle to find some way to survive that did not involve an abdication of my dignity as an intelligent human being. I had been through one unsuccessful marriage, yet I had never known fatherhood or family. What's more and worse, my efforts in the literary vineyard had yet to produce anything resembling the glorious masterpieces I once adumbrated in my artistic visions.

For the first time in his life Ed was not being objective. As Pooky so rightly pointed out, he had known—and given—much joy in life, and had much to be proud of. More importantly, now independently wealthy, and still in the prime of life, he was forever free to do as he pleased. He was simply experiencing that classic mid-life shock, when we realize we're no longer on the way in, but on the way out. While still pondering whether to take Gregory's queen (affording my nephew an early lesson in improvidence) I interjected—

"I'd say five years would be enough to cover all the operas. Especially since your resources are virtually unlimited."

"But that's just one thing," Ed said. "I want to see all of Bergman's films, learn to play the violin, become fluent in Italian, go to Antarctica . . ."

It was beautiful to see Ed's gusto for life. Hemmed in for years by manuals on pension law, his spirit soared with the idea that he would soon retire from monetary pursuits, that his time would be his own. My mother again brought in the wisdom of the ages.

"If there's anything you want to do, you'd better do it now. That's what I've always said."

Of course, I reflected, Mom won't have the option of physical immortality. She's sure to be gone well before the death-cheating technologies come on line. We all felt it, but no one said it. Nor did we dwell on the fact that Pooky, Dan and I all lack the prodigious financial resources to undergo the constant consultations and supplements needed to procure eternal life. I thought of an old church song:

> *I've got a mother, a sister and a brother,*
> *Who have passed this way before,*
> *I am determined to go and see them, Good Lord,*
> *Over on the other shore . . .*

I didn't share my metaphsyical musings with the family.

My Immortal Brother

Ed had dismissed belief in the supernatural as so much mumbo-jumbo while still an adolescent. Nor were the rest of our clan particularly inclined toward spiritual matters. But what if there was some kind of great yonder, where we could all gather together again, without worry or care? Did Ed really want to take a chance on missing it? Somewhere along the way I had also left behind our Baptist upbringing, but I was skeptical that you could get to Kingdom Come without some kind of Judgment Day. It seemed necessary for simple symmetry's sake, if nothing else. Just as light needs dark, or day needs night, any life worthy of the name seems to require the constant awareness of our impending doom.

Noticing Gregory squirming in his chair—dying, himself, with impatience for me to move, so he could plow ahead to victory—I decided not to take his queen. Instead, I advanced one of my pawns.

His eyes lit up like signal flares.

The luncheon was breaking up, and Gregory came a step closer to checkmating me. I could have allowed him to take my king, but that would have been going too far. As we cleared the board, he was chiefly concerned about knowing who had won. "So that was a tie?" he asked. "More or less," I said. "You've taken more of my pieces, so we could say that you were ahead." "So I won," he concluded with satisfaction, more concerned with one present victory than the distant hereafter.

I have spoken to my friends about Ed's impending deathless state. I even received a call from one of my nephews, Ed's eldest who, like me, couldn't quite wrap his mind around it. It's pretty heady stuff, my brother having discovered a way to disarm the grim reaper—as if the spectral presence that has haunted humanity down the ages were no more threatening than Boo O'Hara, or some thug in a parking lot. But Ed is nothing if not a high achiever. And the simple fact is, he has always been, and always will be (medical technologies notwithstanding) among the immortals to me. I'm touched, in any event, by the way he shared his plans with the family, and I know he'd like nothing more than for all of us to remain here on earth with him and Deirdre through the centuries. If there is a great beyond, which I'm thoroughly counting on, I'm going to miss him there. Deirdre, too. But I'm banking on the conviction that a few hundred years of opera, violin and Italian will be enough for anyone; that, sooner or later, we'll all be together again.

The Way We Do Things (1999)

"THAT WAS THE BEST father's day I've ever had."

They were the old man's words, as we stood in the foyer of his townhouse, hugging and joking with the kids. But why did he say that? The usual people were there: Ed and Deirdre, their sons and daughters; Pooky and Dan, and baby Todd; my father, and his ladyfriend, Debbie. I had arrived after a morning shift at the radio station.

The old man was on the patio grilling steaks; I smelled the charring meat when I got out of the car. I stood at the gate of the high, latticed fence that surrounds his small back yard. My father's back was to me. He was turning steaks and chatting with Alice, one of Deirdre's daughters. Beyond them, in the rec room, I could see the rest of my family. I waved an arm over my head, trying to get someone's attention.

Finally William, Ed's younger son, noticed me. He wore a loose-fitting Hawaiian shirt. He opened the sliding glass door and came across the patio, his solid shoulders swaying like the high school wrestler he was.

"What's the matter, Un-cool," he said when he got to the gate, a touch of wry laughter in his voice. "You seem to be rather locked out."

William's cheekiness didn't bother me, nor his use of my longstanding moniker: both were marks, not only of my nephew's charming wit, but also of a lifelong relationship of affectionate closeness. Besides, he was already throwing the several bolts that secure the rear entrance to my father's suburban stronghold. I said hello to the old man and Alice and gave them each a hug. As my father took steaks off the grill, Alice arranged them on a plate with a paper towel on it. She, like my other nephews and nieces, calls my father "Grandy," a moniker with no precedent on my—the Burns side—of the family. In the rec room, the rest of our extended clan was draped over sofas and chairs, or lying on the floor. My kid sister—Pooky—was nursing baby Todd in the yellow recliner by the sliding glass doors. His arms were wrapped around her breast like an astronaut grappling a space capsule, his weightless body floating across her midriff.

"Hey, Bro," Ed called out from across the room.

I made a general wave as I removed my shoes.

"I've got that power of attorney for you. It's upstairs on the coffee table. You might want to get it, because it keeps getting moved around."

My brother Ed is a lawyer.

"Power of attorney," Pooky chirped, "what's that?"

"That's a document that will let Ed get into my bank accounts, or deal with any of my other affairs, while I'm overseas."

I was planning an extended sojourn in Portugal.

"I could have done that," Pooky said plaintively, wanting to be helpful.

I sensed an opportunity to tease my kid sister. "The problem," I said, "is it's generally good to have someone who can leave the house if they need to." To soften the ribbing, I placed a hand on her shoulder, by way of greeting, and squeezed. She laughed, as a good sport as always, and Ed made a crack or two along the same lines; that is, that since the birth of baby Todd, my sister had been under virtual house arrest, her jailer a tyrannical, ravenous, breast-hugging three-month-old.

I patted Pooky's shoulder, knowing we were touching a nerve, but she just kept smiling. I looked down and greeted her husband, Dan, who sat on the floor with his back against the sofa. I wondered how he felt, floating in this in-law stew, in-laws who teased or doted on his wife and now threatened to co-opt his firstborn. He stared ahead, smiling weakly at our jokes, nodding slightly. He looked almost as tired as Pooky.

After dinner we discussed the wedding of Prince Edward Windsor, the son of Queen Elizabeth, to Sophie Rys-Jones.

"Show you how bored I am," Pooky started up, "I watched the whole thing on TV the other day."

"That's not so absurd," I said, I, too, wanting to be helpful.

She was at one end of the big maple table in my father's dining room, holding baby Todd across her bosom. On her plate were the spent cobs of three ears of corn she had just devoured like a stray cat.

"There were three hundred and sixty-five thousand beads on her gown," she took up again, now in a surprisingly serviceable impersonation of the BBC commentator. "She wore the Queen's tiara"—and then in her normal voice—"I guess that's her something borrowed. . . ."

My father made small nods while she spoke, emitting low "mm-hms" with each one, indicating he'd seen the coverage, waiting for a chance to chime in . . .

"You know they went on about every little detail," Pooky went on. "This commentator guy goes, something like, 'I say, Judy (Brit accent again) isn't it rather odd that Charles is wearing a gray suit? I don't believe that's customary, is it?'"

We were all amused by her accent, even Ed's eldest Dirk, whose long limbs were splayed before his chair in his standard pose of casual disinterest. It was also encouraging, and I think everyone felt a pleasant sense of relief, to see Pooky, so lately beset by the trials of motherhood, having a good time.

"And what's this Queen Mother thing?" she blurted now, her face lit up with puzzled hilarity. "Who *is* the Queen Mother, anyway?"

"She's the mother of the Queen," my father said matter-of-factly, also wanting to help. He had always referred to Pooky as "little princess."

"She was the queen before Elizabeth," he added.

"Then why isn't she still queen?" Pooky asked, bewildered.

The old man cocked his head, a gesture that meant he was about to get funny: a moment that, in some unspoken way, we had all been waiting for . . .

"Well," he began, also affecting a British accent, puckering his lips so his voice sounded like it were being forced through a tea strainer, "when the Queen Mother—Mummy—started having trouble finding the castle, they thought it best she step down . . ."

Pooky blurted a laugh, releasing the comic tension she had initiated when she screwed up her face and asked, "Who *is* the Queen Mother, anyway?"

As if she knew. . . .

"She was found wandering into pharmacies," the old man started up again, before switching to the Queen Mother voice and asking, "Can someone please show me to the throne room?"

Everyone laughed, and over the subsiding guffaws Pooky put in, in a disparaging tone, "The ring didn't even fit her finger. He had to shove it past her knuckle!"

"And those dumbbells at CBS," my father stated flatly, "kept putting up Princess Di's picture every three minutes."

There was no bitterness in his voice; that people in the media were dumbbells was a fact the old man had long since grown into.

"There's a striking similarity between the two, don't you think?" Pooky resumed in her BBC commentator voice.

"That was in bad taste, wasn't it," I remarked, "constantly showing Di's photo during the wedding? I mean, she's barely in the grave. . . ."

"That was nothing," Pooky said. "After that, this commentator guy goes" (commentator voice again), "But if you could see the two of them walking away from you, there'd be no mistaking them . . ."

Pooky looked at Dad—cueing him, as it were. He was already chuckling.

"Yes," he began, best King's English, "Sophie is decidedly pear-shaped, while Diana was quite svelte. . . ."

We all broke up, and young Dirk's horsy laugh echoed around the room. His father—my brother Ed—announced that he was leaving to take William to his summer job, caddying at a local country club. After they made their way out the door, we carried on . . .

"Will Sophie be queen next?" Pooky innocently asked now, genuinely intrigued by the succession to the British throne.

"Nooo," my father said, "Prince Charles' sons are next in line." He went on to describe the mechanics of the royal succession in a not unworkmanlike way. I was impressed how the old man, who left school after the tenth grade, managed to keep himself informed about the world.

"So, Michael's next in line," he concluded.

"What about Charles?" someone said.

"He's out."

"Why?"

"It's because of his affair with Camilla, isn't it?" Pooky asked.

"Not exactly," the old man began, visibly trying to sort it

out. "It's actually because he's divorced."

"Is divorce a bar to the British crown?" I asked skeptically, rifling my memory for an historic precedent.

"Sure," the old man insisted, "that's why Henry the Eighth had to kill all his wives. He couldn't divorce them."

I didn't attempt to correct the inaccuracy (Henry famously divorced Catherine of Aragon, of course, so that he could marry Anne Boleyn). We were all getting out of our depths, but the important thing is, we were having fun. Still, the one-time history major in me couldn't resist prying for some rational explanation, and I brought up the abdication of Edward VIII for Wallis Simpson.

"Well, she was a commoner," the old man riffed.

"Sophie's a commoner too," Pooky added triumphantly. "She's got her own public relations firm." (Prior to baby Todd's birth, Pooky was an account manager with a large advertising agency.)

"Is Camilla noble?" I asked. I don't keep up with the tabloids.

"She's a ho," Pooky said.

"Is that why Charles is out?" young Dirk put in.

"I think he'd have trouble with Parliament," I ventured, more or less improvising myself.

"I think it's because she's a ho-bag," Pooky repeated, delighted with herself.

I thought of my brother Ed. I knew we would not be having this conversation, not in the manner we were having it, in any case, had he not left the gathering. A rational-minded lawyer to the bone, he would have found some way, if only by his mere presence, to keep us focused on verifiable facts. His wife Deirdre smiled good-naturedly, but she didn't join, any more than Ed would have, in the crazy bazaar of conjecture going on around her. Nor did Pooky's husband, Dan, join in. Alice and Kristen, Deirdre's daughters from her first marriage, had migrated to the living room, where they appeared to be discussing some teenage dilemma in private.

"I still don't see why Sophie can't be queen next," Pooky said, "since Elizabeth is queen, and Mummy before her…"

"It's a male thing, baby," I said.

"That's not right," she rejoined emphatically. Her identification with the women of the House of Windsor was palpable. She had always been "little princess," but could she never be queen? Even now that she was a mother?

"You see, Sis," I said, "the British crown passes through the male line."

"That sucks," she said with resigned, if indignant, finality.

The old man started in again about how Mummy was captured on worldwide television eating mints at the ceremony. And so we went on for some time, discussing the Queen's wealth, who would get it when she died, the many castles she owned, and where the newlyweds would live. We were caught up in the storied lives of these people, relating to their emoluments, as well as their predicaments, almost as if they were our own.

II.

Before dinner Deirdre and I had sat at one end of the big maple table in a momentary bubble of silence. Debbie was in the kitchen finishing the corn on the cob; my father was still at the grill; everyone else was in the basement.

Her father had died a few weeks earlier. He had been a submarine commander until his retirement, many years previous, and had been buried with full military honors at Pensacola. Deirdre flew to her parents' home in Alabama during the final days of his illness. My brother Ed drove the kids down for the funeral. I had seen Deirdre only once since then, when young Dirk graduated high school. There was quite a crowd at the house in Baltimore, but Deirdre kept her chin up and played the wonderful hostess like always.

"I haven't allowed myself time to grieve," she told me, permitting only a bare hint of emotional and physical exhaustion to come through. She had just returned from Alabama, where she had helped her mother cope with a houseful of out-of-town family.

"I felt like I had to be the strong one."

She showed me a spent shell from the military funeral's twenty-one gun salute. It had a dull, brass shine to it. I held it in my hand. The hollow tube was so light, it seemed it might float away. Yet it was something palpable, something to clasp her fingers around until a more fundamental remembrance might take shape.

"It's like nothing I've ever been through," she said.

We could hear Debbie rattling pots in the kitchen.

"It's not so much hard as . . . complicated."

I figured it was damn hard. But she would never let us down by allowing any circumstance, no matter how demanding, shatter the sense of equipoise we'd all come to expect from her.

"Ed and I were sitting on the patio the other day, just watching the birds, and looking at the different flowers that were coming up. And I suddenly realized he's not here anymore to enjoy all of that. He'll never be able to see it again." It was like her to put things in simple, concrete terms. I mentioned the possibility of reincarnation, suggesting he might indeed soon be enjoying life on earth again.

"I know," she said.

We sat in silence for a moment.

"It's been odd, after so many Father's Days, always finding something to give him . . ."

I thought of that spent shell.

"Now I've been thinking of everything he gave me."

III.

After dinner we asked young Dirk about Beach Week. Flush from his high school graduation, he and his friends had rented a house at Nag's Head, North Carolina. Between keg parties and chasing girls, he and his buddies had spent some time in the surf. He was losing the reticence that had marked most of his teen years, a reticence broken only by brief, sardonic quips; and after Pooky drew him out in a nice, aunt-like way, he warmed up to recounting some of his adventures.

"Okay, listen to this . . ." Enlivened by some memory, he swept an arm across the air, preparing the canvas for a new picture . . .

"The beach down there had these, like, sandbars, every hundred feet or so. But in between, the water was really, really deep. So there'd be, like, a sand bar, then some deep water, then another sand bar. Then some more deep water. I think there were, like, six or seven sand bars, and they all had this really deep water between them."

I had only asked how the surf was.

"Anyway, me and my buddy Jake were out there swimming, and at first everything was fine and normal. But then, all of a sudden, it felt like I was swimming harder and harder, but I wasn't getting anywhere . . ."

"There was an undertow," I clarified. My father nodded in agreement.

"I know, I know" Dirk said breathlessly, dismissing my comment with a wave of his hand, anxious to keep his story moving . . .

"So, like I was saying," he went on, "I'm swimming, like, really hard, but I'm not getting anywhere. And me and Jake are way out there. I mean, we're past the fourth or fifth sandbar, like, hundreds of feet from the beach! And I'm thinking, oh shii . . ."

He let his voice trail off before completing the expletive, instead emitting a nervous, throaty laugh. He looked tentatively at my father, half-expecting an admonition, but the old man just smiled and nodded.

"Now I'm starting to get really worried," Dirk went on excitely, "because my arms are getting tired. You know, starting to cramp up a little. I really don't know how long I can keep this up!"

He pantomimed swimming, bobbing his head in gentle undulations, wearily ducking and weaving.

I came in with a little avuncular advice.

"You should have swam parallel to the shore . . ."

Though I spoke perfectly plainly, Dirk paid me no mind. "So, I'm swimming the best I can. . . ." he continued.

"When you're in an undertow, you need to . . ."

"And I'm getting really tired . . ."

". . . swim parallel to the shore, until you get past the undercurrent."

"I'm actually afraid I'm going to drown out there!"

"Listen to your uncle," the old man finally broke in. "He's trying to teach you something."

"I know, I know," Dirk clipped out, even less inclined than before, it seemed, to break the momentum of his tale. We let him continue . . .

"So, I'm really swimming like crazy now. I mean, I'm getting desperate! I'm actually starting to flail a little. And just about then, I hear Jake calling out behind me. He's calling out my name. 'Dirk!' he yells, 'Dirk!' But I don't look around. I'm just concentrating on swimming because, you know, I'm really afraid I'm not going to get out of there alive. But Jake just won't shut up, so, finally, I roll over sideways a bit so I can look back at him.

"And now I see Jake there, about ten feet behind me. And it took a moment to get my head wrapped around it because, the funny thing is, he's vertical. I mean, he's standing up. Not swimming at all!" Dirk stands up from the table himself at this juncture, and with the edge of his hand marks a spot about half-way up his thigh. "And the water," he goes on, "comes up to about, oh, here. Around his, I don't know, his thigh or something."

He looks around the table with a loping gesture, accompanied by that fashionable "Duh" expression on his face.

Pooky bursts out a cackle. "Ha," she says, "you were over the sand bar the whole time, and you didn't even know it! That's pretty funny!"

My father wore a satisfied grin. He had always enjoyed Dirk's sense of humor, and was fond of saying that his winning personality would more than make up for the lack of academic success that had colored his high school career.

"The most important thing in business is people skills," he liked to say.

The old man, a product of rural poverty during the Depression, had retired at the head of a wholesale food business not only by dint of hard work, but also on account of his companionable nature, and a penchant for telling funny stories.

"Man, it was weird," Dirk concluded. He took up his plate and headed toward the kitchen.

IV.

Dirk's father—my brother, Ed—graduated at the top of his law school class. Now he was the managing partner of a rapidly growing firm, and he would soon be financially independent. In him my father's drive, and my mother's practical organizational abilities, had found a companionable marriage. He had set his goals intelligently, and he was now in the process of achieving them, one by one.

His oldest son, defying the old adage about trees and acorns, appeared to be rudderless. Now a high school graduate, he had no plans for the future. His high school failures were not owing to any deficit in intelligence, in my judgment, but to what appeared to be a complete lack of interest in books. On the other hand, he had been exceedingly popular with his classmates, as had been his father. His chief interest was rock n' roll music.

It was no coincidence that rock n' roll was also my brother Ed's greatest enthusiasm, next to his family. When he and I were boys, we would pore lovingly throughout the year at those few pages of the Sears and Roebuck catalogue devoted to guitars and amplifiers. As often as we asked our parents, however, no spangled, glittering, Silvertone electric ever materialized under the Christmas tree. Gifts of that caliber were far outside the family budget during that epoch in our family's history, when my father was still slogging through the gray-collar trenches of the wholesale grocery trade. It was only later, with earnings from summer jobs, that we each managed to buy guitars on our own.

Ed and I both maintained our interest in music as adults and, when young Dirk grew old enough to manage an instrument, my brother bought him a bass guitar. Dirk displayed a ready musical intelligence, and he quickly mastered the bass lines to the classic rock tunes his father enjoyed, and that the Burns clan loved to reproduce together in my brother and Deirdre's basement at family get-togethers.

The Way We Do Things (1999)

Now Dirk wanted me to hear a new band he was fond of.

"Un-cool, you want to hear some of these guys?" He showed me the CD cover.

I can't remember the name of the group. They looked like other bands of the era. There was no CD player in my father's townhouse, so we went out to Dirk's Chevrolet Cavalier: aside from his bass, his most prized possession. Settling into the driver's seat, he deftly slid the CD into the changer.

"Wait'll you hear this, Un-cool. It's really jammin'." He turned up the volume. "Okay, here goes." His normally slack body grew taut, anticipating the first, punchy chords. Then, after ticking off each beat with a quick, precise gesture, he began to slap-plunk a bass across his stomach. The band was indeed decent enough. The guitarists were excellent, the production tight, and the compositions interesting for the genre. I couldn't argue when Dirk said again, "It's really jammin', isn't it?"

I mentioned some bands from the classic rock era that seemed to resonate in the group's music. It was the best I could offer, as I hadn't kept up with popular music for some years. Dirk knew that I preferred classical and jazz, a trait he found incomprehensible, but tolerable, so long as I was willing to run through "Johnny B. Goode" or "Dixie Chicken" with the boys when we all got together.

We spent fifteen minutes discussing Dirk's efforts to form a band of his own.

"That's what I want it to sound like." He pointed to the CD changer. "Just like that."

V.

When Dirk and I returned to the house everyone was in the living room. Kristen and Alice purred over baby Todd in the big recliner. The U.S. Open was on the tube, an annual Father's

Day staple at the old man's place.

Ed had returned.

I sat beside Pooky on one of the long sofas that engulfed the coffee table. She was momentarily free of Todd, and it was like a great weight had been lifted from her.

"How's it going, Sis?" I put an arm around her shoulders.

"*Much* better."

The first months of motherhood had not been easy for my sister. Her maniacal commitment to breast-feeding, combined with her son's voracious appetite, led to chronic lack of sleep and general exhaustion. Added to these difficulties were a painful yeast infection and the isolation of a suburban Mom. I had been concerned on more than one occasion that she was on the verge of cracking up. "It's great you're breast-feeding him," I had ventured at one point, "but not if you end up in the nuthouse."

That's what I said, trying to be funny.

But she was happy today. Everything was fine, and Dan was content. He lay sprawled on the living room floor, captivated by the Open.

The tournament, now in its final round, had come down to a contest between golf greats Payne Stewart and Phil Mickelson. Mickelson's wife was expecting their first child at any moment, and Mickelson had announced that he would leave the course—though this would result in his defaulting the tournament—if she were to go into labor. The commentators referred to these facts frequently, lending a certain drama (beyond that always attendant upon the paramount golf contest of the season) to the event.

My father's photo albums were being passed around. They were full of shots of my siblings and me as children. There were also snapshots of the many friends the old man had made during his long career in the wholesale food business,. Stuffed in the back were a dozen fading Polaroids of a trip he had taken to Mexico with some buddies after he and our mother divorced.

Dan lay across the carpet on his stomach, watching Pinehurst's lush fairways roll across the screen of the big console TV. Deirdre sat serenely in an easy chair. The rest of us were plopped in the couches around the coffee table. Suddenly our attention was drawn to the television. Phil Mickelson had barely missed his par putt on the sixteenth hole, losing the one-stroke lead he had gained over Stewart on the twelfth.

Dan rolled onto his side to address my father.

"Dag," he said, "it was that close!" He pinched his finger and thumb together, leaving just the merest space.

My father and Dan share an enthusiasm for golf, one not shared by the old man's children. But we all sat up to watch, for who could be utterly insensitive to this dramatic moment of sports agony?

"Wow, look at that," young Dirk suddenly yelped. He pointed to a photo album that lay across Pooky's lap.

"Un-cool," he continued, the utterance of my nickname an admonition in itself, "look how skinny you are. Wow!"

Pooky canted the album so that everyone could see.

"That must have been after you went to India," Dirk went on. "I remember that. You were real skinny, and you had this scraggly beard." Dirk would have been about fourteen at the time. I had no idea my appearance had made such an impression on him.

"You were scary," he said. "Yeah, you scared me."

Again our attention was drawn to a clamor from the TV. Stewart and Mickelson were now on the eighteenth green. Mickelson had sunk his par, which meant that Stewart would need a birdie to win the tournament. He faced an eighteen-foot, uphill putt on a wildly undulating surface.

Stewart was the old man's favorite. Brash, even abrasive in his younger years, he had mellowed with the approach of middle age. More important to my father, he was a guy who had always displayed a lot of "personality."

He sighted carefully down the shaft of the putter.

He stepped around to the ball.

He tapped it, deliberately and firmly.

The ball went in the hole.

The crowd erupted in wild cheers. The commentators began to yak a mile a minute. And in my father's living room, I felt a certain lift. There was a sense of unspoken possibilities, like when a space mission rocket achieves ignition and begins to rise from its launching pad in billowing white clouds.

The old man hooted.

We were all happy.

Stewart's caddy ran onto the green and threw himself upon the champion.

"God, look at the caddy," Dirk bellowed, overcome by incredulous hilarity. "He's even got his legs wrapped around him!"

Indeed, Stewart's caddy was attached to the golfer like a giant barnacle.

Mickelson looked crestfallen.

In the winner's circle Stewart seemed stunned. His face was breaking up, like we were losing reception. But the signal was perfectly clear; no, it was Stewart himself who was disintegrating. He didn't know what was happening. He had just won the U.S. Open with an eighteen-foot putt on the last green.

The commentator was talking with Mickelson.

"Phil, we understand you'd decided to quit the field if your wife went into labor. That must have been a tough decision."

Mickelson nodded vaguely. He looked as dazed as Stewart.

They led him over to the winner's circle, where Stewart thanked the Lord for all the blessings He had bestowed upon him, the latest being the U.S. Open golf championship. Stewart put one arm around his wife's shoulders, the other around Mickelson.

"You made the decision to be there for her," Stewart blubbered, "that's the important thing. I was there when our daughter was born," he added wistfully. Tears brimmed in his eyes.

Mickelson appeared alarmed, though whether at Stewart's emotionalism, which threatened to exceed all bounds of normal post-event sports talk; at having lost the U.S. Open by a hair's breadth; or at the thought of imminent fatherhood, it wasn't clear.

"You'll have your baby," Stewart blubbered.

Consolation prize for losing the Open?

"You'll have your baby," he repeated, hugging Mickelson roundly.

VI.

"That was the best Father's Day I've ever had," the old man said, as we stood in the foyer, hugging and joking with the kids . . ."